9

D1043256

THE WOMAN
WITH THE BOUQUET

Eric-Emmanuel Schmitt

THE WOMAN
WITH THE BOUQUET

*Translated from the French
by Alison Anderson*

Europa
editions

Europa Editions
116 East 16th Street
New York, N.Y. 10003
www.europaeditions.com
info@europaeditions.com

Translation by Alison Anderson
Original title: *La rêveuse d'Ostende*
Translation copyright © 2010 by Europa Editions

This work has been published thanks to the support from the
French Ministry of Culture – Centre National du Livre
Ouvrage publié avec le concours du
Ministère français chargé de la Culture – Centre National du Livre

Library of Congress Cataloging in Publication Data is available
ISBN 978-1-933372-81-5

Schmitt, Eric-Emmanuel
The Woman with the Bouquet

Book design by Emanuele Ragnisco
www.mekkanografici.com

Prepress by Plan.ed
www.plan-ed.it

Printed in Canada

CONTENTS

THE DREAMER
FROM OSTEND

I believe I've never known anyone who proved to be as different from her appearance as Emma Van A.

The first time we met, she merely seemed a fragile, discreet woman, with neither depth nor conversation, so banal you'd think her doomed to oblivion. And yet, because one day I touched upon her reality, she will never cease to haunt me: intriguing, imperious, brilliant, paradoxical, inexhaustible, she has caught me for all eternity in the web of her charm.

Certain women are traps into which you fall. Sometimes you do not want to get out of those traps. Emma Van A. has ensnared me.

It all began during a timid, cool month of March, in Ostend. I had always dreamt about Ostend.

When I travel, names lure me before places do. Standing higher than steeples, words ring out from afar, easily heard thousands of miles away, sending sounds that suggest images.

Ostend . . .

Consonants and vowels draw a map, build walls, specify an atmosphere. When a small town wears the name of a saint, my fantasy constructs it around its church; the moment the word evokes a forest—Boisfort—or fields—Champigny—green invades the narrow streets; if a certain material is referred to—Pierrefonds—my mind scratches against the rough casting in order to exalt the stone; and if it evokes a miracle—Dieulefit—then I imagine a city clinging to a rugged peak, overlooking the countryside. When I approach the town, before all else I have an appointment with the name.

I had always dreamt about Ostend.

I could have happily gone on dreaming about it, without going there, had a sentimental misadventure not forced me out on the road. Flee! Leave behind a city—Paris—saturated with memories of a love that was no more. Quickly, a change of scene, of climate . . .

The North seemed a good solution because we had never been there together. As I unfolded a map, I was immediately hypnotized by six letters inscribed on the blue that represented the North Sea: Ostend. Not only did the sound of it captivate me, but I remembered that a friend had a good address for a place to stay. After a few phone calls, everything was arranged, my room at the pension was reserved, my luggage was piled in the car, and I was on my way to Ostend, as if my fate were waiting for me there.

Because the word began with an O of surprise, then grew softer with the *s,* it anticipated the sensation of bedazzlement as I stood on a sand beach stretching to infinity . . . because I could hear the word "tender" and not "tend," I pictured streets in pastel colors beneath a tranquil sky. Because its linguistic roots suggested to me that it was a town "situated in the West," I imagined houses clustered by the sea, reddened with an eternal setting sun.

Arriving there at night, I did not really know what to think. While for certain elements, the reality of Ostend did coincide with my dream of Ostend, it also forced some brutal realizations upon me: although the municipality was indeed at the end of the earth, in Flanders, built between a sea of waves and a sea of fields, and it did have a vast beach and a nostalgic break-water, it also showed to me the extent to which the Belgians had defaced their coastline on the pretext of sharing it with the greatest number of people. There were row upon row of apartment buildings taller than ocean liners, housing that was neither tasteful nor distinctive, but which corresponded to what was considered profitable real estate, and I discovered an urban chaos that spoke eloquently of the greed of entrepreneurs eager to get their hands on the money of the middle classes as they enjoyed their paid vacations.

Fortunately, the dwelling where I had rented one floor was a survivor from the 19th century, a villa constructed during the reign of Leopold II, the builder king. Very ordinary for its time, it was now exceptional. Set among recent buildings that incarnated a total lack of geometrical inventiveness, simple boxes divided into floors, which in turn were divided into apartments, apartments blocked off by horrible windows of smoked glass, all symmetrical—so rational as to leave you disgusted forever with rationality—my building remained a solitary witness to a desire for architecture; it had taken time to adorn itself, varying the size and rhythm of its apertures, venturing forward with a balcony here, a terrace there, or a winter garden, daring to use high windows, and low ones, and medium sized ones, or even corner windows, then, like a woman who draws a beauty spot on her forehead, taking sudden delight in sporting an *oeil-de-boeuf* beneath the slate roof.

A redheaded woman in her fifties with a broad face covered in red blotches was standing in the open door.

"What do you want?" she asked in a friendly but offhand manner.

"Is this indeed the residence of Madame Emma Van A.?"

"That's right," she grunted in a rustic Flemish accent that emphasized her sinister looking aspect.

"I've rented your second floor for two weeks. My friend from Brussels must have informed you."

"Well yes, of course! We've been expecting you! I'll tell my aunt. Come in, please, just come on in."

With her rough hands, she grabbed my cases, set them down

in the hall and pushed me into the living room with gruff ami-
ability.

The silhouette of a frail woman stood out against the
window: she was seated in a wheelchair, facing a sky that drank
the dark ink of the sea.

"Aunt Emma, here's your lodger."

Emma Van A. swung around and considered me.

Where other people, in order to please, become lively when
they greet someone, she set to studying me gravely. She was very
pale, her skin more worn by the years than by wrinkles, her hair
divided between black and white to form a whole that was not
gray but two distinct colors, with contrasting highlights. And
her long face rested on a slender neck: was it her age? was it an
attitude? Her head was cocked to one side, her ear above her
left shoulder, her chin raised toward her right shoulder, in such
a way that, given her sideways attention, she seemed to be listening rather than observing.

I had to break the silence: "Good morning, Madame, I am
delighted to have found a place to stay in your home."

"Are you a writer?"

I understood the implication of her prior examination: she
was wondering if I had the proper physique to write novels.

"Yes."

She sighed, as if relieved. Visibly, it was my position as an
author that had made her decide to open her home to me.

Behind me her niece understood that the intruder had
passed his entrance examination, so she blared like a trombone,
"Okay, I'm off to finish preparing the rooms, right, it'll be ready
in five minutes."

As she was leaving the room, Emma Van A. gazed devotedly
at her the way one gazes at a faithful but stubborn dog.

"You must excuse her, sir, my niece has not learned to speak
politely to strangers in French. You see, in Dutch we are much
less formal."

"It's a pity not to learn the pleasures of French formality."

"The greatest pleasure would be to use a language where it's not an issue, no?"

Why had she said such a thing? Was she afraid I might become too familiar? I remained on my feet, somewhat awkward. She invited me to sit down.

"It's odd. I've spent my life surrounded by books but I've never met a writer."

A glance around me confirmed what she had said: thousands of volumes filled the shelves of the living room, spilling over even into the dining room. To allow me to have a better look, she glided through the furniture in her wheelchair, as silent as a shadow, and lit some lamps that glowed faintly.

Although I enjoy nothing more than the company of printed paper, her library put me ill at ease, for a reason I was unable to determine. The volumes were very handsome, meticulously bound in leather or canvas, the titles and names of the authors engraved in gold letters; all different sizes, there were lined up in varying ways, with neither excessive disorder nor symmetry, according to a rhythm that was proof of constant good taste, and yet . . . Are we so used to original editions that a bound collection is disconcerting? Was I suffering because I saw no sign of my favorite dust jackets? I found it difficult to pinpoint my disquiet.

"You will forgive me, I haven't read your novels," she said, mistaken as to the reasons for my confusion.

"Please don't apologize. Nobody can know everything. Moreover, I don't even expect it of the people I see regularly."

Relieved, she stopped shaking the coral bracelet she had around her thin wrist and smiled at the walls.

"And yet I devote all my time to reading. And rereading. Yes, above all. I reread a great deal. You only really discover a masterpiece after the third or fourth reading, don't you agree?"

"And how can you tell something is a masterpiece?"

"I don't skip over the same passages."

She took a garnet leather volume and opened it, a wistful intensity in her gaze.

"*The Odyssey*, for example. I can open it at any page and enjoy it immensely. Do you like Homer, Monsieur?"

"Naturally."

Her irises grew dark, and this suggested to me that she found my answer to be flippant, or even offhand. I struggled therefore to develop a more specific point of view.

"I have often identified with Ulysses, because he turns out to be more crafty than intelligent, he goes home without rushing, and he respects Penelope without disdaining any of the lovely women he meets on his journey. Basically, he has so little virtue, does Ulysses, that I feel close to him. I find him modern."

"How odd to believe in contemporary immorality, it's naïve, too . . . With each generation, young people are under the impression that they are inventing vice: such presumption! What sorts of books do you write?"

"My own books. They don't belong to any particular genre."

"Very good," she concluded, and her professorial tone confirmed that I was passing an exam.

"Would you allow me to give you a copy of one?"

"I . . . did you bring one with you?"

"No. However, I am sure that in the bookstores in Ostend—"

"Yes, bookstores . . ."

She uttered the word as if someone had just reminded her of the existence of an ancient and forgotten thing.

"You know, Monsieur, this library was my father's, he taught literature. I have been living among these publications since my childhood, with no need to add to his collection. There are so many opuscules that I have not yet read. Look, no further than just there behind you, George Sand, Dickens . . . I still have a few volumes of theirs to discover. And Victor Hugo, too."

"The genius of Victor Hugo is that there is always a page of Victor Hugo that one hasn't read."

"Exactly. It reassures me to live like this, watched over, surrounded by giants! That is why there are not a lot of . . . new books, here."

After a moment of hesitation, she had pronounced the words "new books" with caution and regret, articulating them reluctantly, as if they were vulgar, even obscene words. As I listened to her, I realized that it was indeed a commercial term, used to designate an item in fashion, but inappropriate to define a literary work; I also realized that to her eyes I was nothing but an author of "new books," a supplier, in a way.

"But novels by Daudet or Maupassant—weren't they 'new books,' when they came out?" I asked.

"Time has given them their place," she replied, as if I had just said something insolent.

I felt like suggesting that she was the one, now, who seemed to be naïve, but as I felt I did not have the right to contradict my hostess, I merely tried to determine why I felt ill at ease: this library did not breathe, it had frozen into a museum forty or fifty years earlier, and it would never again evolve for as long as its owner refused to allow an injection of new blood into it.

"Forgive my indiscretion, Monsieur: are you alone?"

"I came here to recover from a separation."

"Oh, I am sorry . . . very sorry . . . I've hurt you, bringing it up . . . oh, forgive me."

Her warmth, her dismay, her sudden nervousness emphasized her sincerity: she really was cross with herself for having plunged my mind into a bucket of bad memories. She mumbled, distraught, "Ostend is the perfect place for a broken heart."

"Do you think so? Do you think I'll get over it here?"

She stared at me with a frown.

"Get over it? You want to get over it?"

"Heal my wounds, yes."

"And do you think you will manage?"

"Yes, I think so."

"That's strange," she murmured, staring at me intently, as if she had never seen me before.

The last steps of the staircase vibrated with her niece's weight as she arrived, breathless, crossing her short arms over her shapeless chest, to declaim victoriously, "Okay, you can move in! All the rooms up there are yours. You can choose your bedroom. Follow me, if you please."

"Gerda will show you the way, my good man. Since my health problems, I can only take care of the ground floor. Which means you can have the entire floor upstairs: you'll be comfortable, there. Help yourself to any books you find, just remember to put them back in place."

"Thank you."

"Gerda will bring your breakfast in the morning, if you don't get up too early."

"Half past nine would suit me."

"Perfect. A good evening, then, Monsieur, and enjoy your stay."

Why did I have a sudden flash of inspiration? I sensed that she was the type of woman who expected me to kiss her hand. I had aimed correctly: no sooner did I approach her than she held out her wrist, and I bent over it in customary fashion.

Her niece watched us as if we were two clowns, shrugged her shoulders, grabbed the suitcases and began to climb up the wobbly staircase of varnished wood.

As I was leaving the living room, Emma Van A.'s voice stopped me: "Monsieur, I have been thinking about what you just said, that you thought your wounds would heal. Please don't be misled by my reaction: it was approval. I do wish it for you. I would be very happy for your sake."

"Thank you, Madame Van A., I too would be very happy."

"Because if you do recover, it means that in any case it wasn't worth it."

My jaw dropped.

She examined me intensely then declared in a peremptory tone, "From a truly essential love, one does not recover."

At which point, her hands went to the wheels of her chair, and in three seconds, she was back by the window, just as I had found her when I arrived.

Upstairs, I discovered the rooms were tastefully, elaborately decorated, with a feminine touch, and the old-fashioned aspect merely added to the charm.

After I had looked around, I chose the "blue titmice" bedroom, so named because of the fabric on the walls, a sort of faintly Japanese cotton canvas whose faded hues conveyed a subtle refinement. As I was settling in, I struggled to clear a spot amidst all the knickknacks to put my own things, but the décor, like a baroque sculpture made of shells, only made sense by virtue of its profusion.

Gerda recommended a few restaurants, entrusted me with a set of keys, and left to head off on her bicycle to cover the six miles from here to her home.

I decided to try the inn that was nearest the Villa Circé, and save any walking for the next day. I was already drunk on the sea air, and fell asleep the moment I stretched out under the heavy quilt that covered my bed.

In the morning, after the copious breakfast that Gerda brought me—mushrooms, eggs, potato croquettes—I was not surprised to find Emma Van A. in her place by the window.

As she had not heard me come down, and the daylight was pouring boldly into the room, I could see my landlady's features, and observe her behavior, with greater ease.

Although she was not doing anything, she did not seem idle. Various emotions flickered across her gaze, thoughts tightened then relaxed her forehead, her lips closed around a thousand utterances that sought to escape. Overwhelmed by a rich inner life, Emma Van A. divided her time between the pages of a novel open on her lap and the flow of dreams that invaded her the moment she raised her head toward the bay. It was as if there were two separate ships sailing by: the ship of her thoughts and the ship of the book; from time to time, when she lowered her eyelids, their wakes mingled for a moment, wedding their waves, then her own ship continued on its way. She read in order not to find herself alone and adrift, she read not to fill a spiritual void but to accompany an all too powerful capacity to create. Literature like bloodletting, to avoid fever . . .

Emma Van A. must have been very beautiful, even as an old woman. However, a recent illness—a cerebral hemorrhage, according to Gerda—had relegated her from antique store to junk shop. Since that time her muscles had melted, her body was no longer slim but thin. She seemed so light that you could imagine her bones to be porous, to the point of breaking. Her joints were ravaged by arthritis, and this made her gestures difficult, yet she seemed not to notice, for she was burning with life. Her eyes were still remarkable: large, a faded blue, a blue where the clouds of the north passed over.

My greeting startled her from her meditation, and she gazed at me, distraught. At that moment, I would have qualified her as anguished. Then a smile came, a real smile, not a trace of hypocrisy, a ray of light in an ocean climate.

"Good morning. Did you sleep well?"

"So well that I can't even remember. I'm going to explore Ostend."

"How I envy you . . . enjoy your day, Monsieur."

I strolled for several hours in Ostend, never staying for more than twenty minutes in the streets away from the shore, always returning to the promenade or the breakwater, like a seagull called by the air of the open sea.

The North Sea was the color of oysters, from the green-brown of the waves to the mother-of-pearl white of the foam; these alternating hues with their gem-like, distilled nuances were restful to me, after my brilliant memories of the Mediterranean with its pure blue and yellow sand, colors as vivid as in a child's drawing. Now these dulled tones evoked the taste of the sea that comes with the delight of eating seafood in a brasserie, and the sea itself was saltier.

Although I had never been to Ostend before, I was rediscovering memories here, and I let childhood sensations lull my mind. My pants rolled up to my knees, I surrendered my feet to the sting of the sand, then the reward of the water. As in the old days, I went into the waves up to mid-calf, fearful of venturing any further. As in the old days, I felt how small I was, beneath an infinite sky, facing the infinite waves.

There were not many people around me. Old folk. Is it for this reason that old people appreciate the seashore? Because when they are swimming, they are ageless? Because they rediscover humility, the simple pleasures of childhood? Because, while buildings and businesses record the passage of time, the sand and the waves remain virginal, eternal, innocent? The seashore remains a secret garden over which time has no hold.

I bought some shrimps that I ate standing up, dipping them into a tub of mayonnaise, then I continued on my stroll.

When I got back to the Villa Circé, at around six o'clock, I was drunk on the wind and the sun, and my head was full of reveries.

Emma Van A. turned to me with a smile on seeing my joyfully inebriated state, and she asked with a knowing air, "Well, how was your exploration of Ostend?"

"Fascinating."

"How far did you go?"

"To the port. Because, quite honestly, I could not settle here without sailing."

"Oh, yes? You would only stay here on condition that you could leave again? A typical male remark."

"You're quite right. Men become sailors and women . . ."

". . . the wives of sailors! And then their widows."

"What is one waiting for, when one spends an entire life above a port at the ends of the earth?"

She was aware of how incongruous my statement was, and she gazed warmly at me, without answering, encouraging me to go on. And so I did: "Is one waiting for a departure?"

She shook her shoulders to rule out that hypothesis.

"Or a return, rather?"

Her large gray irises held my gaze. I thought I glimpsed a shadow of a pain, but her voice was firm, denying it: "One remembers, Monsieur, one remembers."

Then she turned her face to the open sea. Again she was so absorbed that I was no longer there; she stared out into the distance the way I would contemplate the blank page, and in her dreaming she ventured out there resolutely.

What was she remembering? Nothing under this roof spoke of her past, everything belonged to previous generations—books, furniture, paintings. It was as if she had come here like a magpie with a stolen treasure, and she had put it down, and had only bothered to replace the curtains and the wallpaper.

Upstairs, I asked her niece, "Gerda, your aunt has told me that she spends her days remembering the past. In your opinion, what is she remembering?"

"I have no idea. She didn't work. She was an old maid."

"Really?"

"Yep, for sure. We never saw no men around Aunt Emma, poor thing. Ever. The family knows that. Know what, as soon as you say gentleman or marriage, she snaps shut like a clam."

"A broken engagement? A fiancé who died in the war? Some disappointment she thinks of as her tragedy, and that she's still nostalgic about?"

"Not even! Back in the days when there were more of us in the family, uncles and aunts tried to introduce suitable suitors. Oh yes. Very acceptable fiancés. One fiasco after the other, Monsieur, can you believe it?"

"It's odd . . ."

"To stay on her own? Yes indeed! I know I couldn't . . . I may not have married the most handsome man round these parts, but at least he's there, he gave me children. A life like the one my aunt has had? I'd rather commit suicide right away."

"And yet she doesn't seem unhappy."

"You got to give her credit: she doesn't complain. Even now, when her strength is leaving her, and her savings have melted like butter, she doesn't complain, does she now! No, she turns to the window, she smiles, she dreams. Basically, it's not much of a life she's lived, but she's had her dreams . . ."

Gerda was right. Emma lived elsewhere, not among us. Wasn't there something about the way she carried her head, her oblique face on her long slender neck that made it tilt to one side, that gave the impression her dreams weighed too heavily with her?

After that discussion, I secretly began to call her the dreamer . . . the dreamer from Ostend.

The next morning, she heard me come down and she pushed her wheelchair over to me.

"Would you like to join me for coffee?"

"With pleasure."

"Gerda! Would you bring us two cups, please."

For my benefit, she whispered: "Her coffee is like dishwater, so weak it wouldn't arouse a newborn baby."

Gerda proudly brought us two steaming cups, as if our desire to chat over her brew paid homage to her culinary talents.

"Madame Van A., I have been quite upset by what you suggested the first evening."

"What was that?"

"I have recovered quickly from the affair that drove me away from Paris: so I did not lose a great deal by putting an end to it. If you remember, you had asserted that one can only get over something if it is not important; on the other hand, one never recovers from an important love."

"I once saw lightning strike a tree. I felt very close to the tree. There is a moment when one burns, one burns up, as it were, it's intense, marvelous. Afterwards, all that is left is ash."

She turned to the sea.

"And no one has ever seen a tree struck by lightning, even if it survives, turn back into an entire tree."

I had the sudden impression that this woman in her wheel-chair was that tree, rooted to the earth . . .

"I get the feeling you are talking to me about yourself," I said gently.

She shuddered. An abrupt anxiety, akin to panic, caused her hands to shake, and her breath came more rapidly. To regain her composure, she picked up her cup, drank from it, scorched her lips, and fussed that it was too hot.

I acted as if I believed her little charade, and I cooled her coffee for her by adding some water.

Once she had recovered, I went ahead all the same: "I want you to know I'm not asking anything of you, Madame Van A.; I respect your privacy, I won't try to invade it in any way."

She swallowed and stared at me as if to test my sincerity; I withstood her scrutiny. Convinced, she eventually cocked her head and murmured in a changed tone of voice, "Thank you."

The time had come for me to give her one of my books—I had bought it the day before, and now I took it from my rear pocket.

"Here you are, I've brought you the novel I find the most accomplished. It would make me very happy if you would read it at some point and share your thoughts with me."

She stopped me, as if stunned.

"Me? But . . . that's impossible."

She lifted her her hands to her heart.

"You understand, I've only read the classics. I don't read . . ."

"New books?"

"That's it, recent publications. I am waiting."

"What are you waiting for?"

"For the author's reputation to be confirmed, for his work to be considered worthy of belonging in a real library, for—"

"For him to die, is that it?"

It came out in spite of myself. I found Emma Van A.'s bad grace with regard to my gift revolting.

"Well then, say it: the best authors are the dead ones! I assure you, it will happen to me, too. One day, I will be consecrated by my ultimate demise and perhaps the next morning you will read me!"

Why such resentment? What difference did it make whether this old maid admired me or not? Why did I feel the need for her to be interested in me?

She sat up straight in her chair, trying to raise herself as high as she could, and although she was lower than me, she looked me up and down: "Monsieur, given my age, and my repeated strokes, do not be presumptuous: in all likelihood I shall leave this earth before you do, and soon. And my disappearance will confer no talent upon me. No more than yours will on you, for that matter."

Her wheelchair spun around; she wove her way among the furniture in the library.

"It is sad to say but we have to accept it: we shall not meet."

She stopped the wheels by the picture window that looked out on the waves.

"It sometimes happens that two people who were meant to set each other ablaze do not experience the great passion for which they were destined because one is too young, and the other too old."

And she added, her voice broken, "It is a great pity, for I should have liked to read you . . ."

She was sincerely remorseful. Honestly, this woman turned my thoughts inside out. I went up to her.

"Madame Van A., it was grotesque of me to get carried away like that, silly to bring this present, and hateful to want to impose it on you. Forgive me."

She turned to me and I saw tears in her eyes, usually so dry.

"I would like to devour your book but I cannot."

"Why not?"

"What if I do not like it?"

Just the thought of it made her shudder with horror. There was something moving about such extreme behavior. I smiled to her. She noticed and returned my smile.

"It would be dreadful: you are such a good person."

"If I were a bad writer, would you no longer think me a good person?"

"No, you would become ridiculous. And as I have such a high opinion of literature, I could not bear for you to be mediocre."

Integrity, such integrity, too much integrity: she vibrated with sincerity.

I wanted to laugh. Why such anguish over a few pages? Our predicament suddenly aroused a bemused tenderness.

"Let's not get angry, Madame Van A. I will take back my novel, and we'll talk about something else."

"Even that is not possible."

"What is not possible?"

"To speak. I cannot tell you whatever I want."

"What's to stop you?"

She prevaricated, looked for help all around her, scanning the shelves to try to find support, almost found an answer, stopped, and then said, exhausted, "My own self."

She sighed, and repeated her answer, distressed, "Yes, my own self . . ."

Her gaze suddenly held mine and with a burst of hopeless energy she said, "You know, I was young once, I was attractive."

Why was she telling me this? What did it have to do with our discussion? Consequently, I stood there with my mouth open.

She insisted, nodding her head this way and that. "Oh yes, I was ravishing. And I was loved!"

"I'm sure you were."

Incensed, she looked me up and down.

"No, you don't believe me!"

"Yes, I do . . ."

"It doesn't matter. I don't care what other people think about me or what they thought about me. Not only do I not care, but it is my fault if people spread untruths about me. I was the cause of them."

"What sort of gossip have they been spreading about you, Madame Van A.?"

"Well nothing, actually."

A pause.

"Nothing. Absolutely nothing."

She shrugged.

"Gerda hasn't talked to you?"

"About what?"

"About this nothing. My family thinks that my life has been empty. Confess . . ."

"Uh . . ."

"There, you see, she told you just that! My life is nothing. And yet, my life has been very rich. It's wrong to call it nothing."

I went up to her.

"Would you like to tell me about it?"

"No. I promised."

"Sorry?"

"I promised to keep it a secret."

"To whom? To what?"

"If I reply, I shall already begin to betray . . ."

She confused me utterly: inside this ancient damsel there burned a strong, sturdy temperament, inhabited by rage and a sharp intelligence, using words like daggers.

She turned to me.

"I was loved, you know. As almost no one ever is. And I loved. Just as much. Oh, yes, so much so that if it were possible . . ."

Her eyes clouded over.

I placed my hand on her shoulder to encourage her.

"It's not forbidden to tell a love story."

"To me, it is. Because the people involved are too important."

Her hands slapped her knees, as if she were imposing silence upon those who wanted to speak.

"What would have been the point of keeping silent all these years if now I break my silence? Well? All my efforts, all these years, reduced to nothing?"

Her knotty fingers seized the wheels of her chair and gave a forceful shove, and she left the room to shut herself in her bedroom.

On coming out of the Villa Circé, I ran into Gerda on the sidewalk, busy sorting garbage into different bins for recycling.

"Are you sure that your aunt did not have a great love in her life?"

"'Course I'm sure, you bet. We teased her about it a lot. If there had been something, she would have told us ages ago, for sure, just to get us to leave her alone!"

Making a terrible racket, with her foot she squashed three plastic bottles so thoroughly they were the size of a cork.

"Allow me to differ with you, Gerda, I'm absolutely convinced of it."

"It's easy to see that you earn your living spouting lies! What an imagination!"

Her stubby fingers tore up the cardboard boxes as if they

were sheets of cigarette paper. She suddenly stopped and stared at two seagulls flying overhead.

"Since you're going on about it, I remember there was Uncle Jan. Yes. He was very fond of Aunt Emma. One day he told me the funniest thing: all the men who had tried to court Aunt Emma had gotten the hell out as fast as they could."

"Why?"

"She was forever spouting such nasty things at them."

"She was nasty?"

"That's what he kept saying, Uncle Jan. You can see the result! Nobody would have her."

"If you analyze what your Uncle Jan said, it's more a case that she wouldn't have any of them."

Gerda was struck dumb by this point of view. I continued: "If she was anywhere as demanding with men as she is with writers, it's easy to understand why no one found grace in her eyes. As she never met any who were good enough, she found a way to discourage them. In reality, your aunt wanted to remain independent."

"I suppose," conceded Gerda reluctantly.

"What's to prove that, if she sent them all packing, it wasn't to make it safe for the one man she was protecting, the only one she didn't talk about?"

"Aunt Emma? A double life? Hmm . . . poor woman . . ."

Gerda grunted, skeptical. Her aunt was only interesting to her as a victim, and the only affection she had for her was pity, or even a touch of scorn; the moment you suggested there might be a rational reason or a source of fulfilment behind her behavior, Gerda no longer paid attention. The mystery did not intrigue her, and explanations only did insofar as they were small-minded. Gerda belonged to those people for whom under-standing is a kind of self-abasement, and anything romantic or sublime was so much vapor to her.

I would have liked to plod along all day, but the weather curtailed my excursion. Not only did a nasty wind trouble my concentration, before long, dark low clouds released a downpour with thick, cold drops.

Two hours later, I sought refuge back at the Villa, and when I came in the door, Gerda assailed me, panic in her voice.

"My aunt is in the hospital, she's had an attack!"

I felt guilty: she had been so distraught when I left her that the emotion must have brought on a mild heart attack.

"What do the doctors say?"

"I was waiting until you got back to go to the hospital. Now I'll go."

"Would you like me to come with you?"

"Hey, she's the one who's sick, not me. And have you got a bike? The hospital isn't exactly next door. Wait here. It's better. I'll be back."

I decided to make the most of her absence to explore the living room. In order to calm my anxiety, I studied the contents of the shelves. While there were classics of world literature, there were also complete editions of authors who had had their season of glory, but to whom nobody in the present day showed the slightest veneration. Consequently, I began to meditate on ephemeral successes, and the transitory nature of fame. I felt crucified by such a prospect. Just because I had readers today, would I have any tomorrow? In their stupidity, writers assume they can escape the mortal condition by leaving something behind them; but does that something last? And while I may know how to talk to a reader in the 21st century, what can I know about a reader in the 23rd? And isn't this question itself rather arrogant? Should I not proscribe it? Should I not rid myself of this pretension? Accept the fact that I live in the present, and only in the present, and enjoy what there is without hope of what will be?

Unaware that such thoughts, by analogy, were increasing my anxiety regarding Emma's health, I lapsed into a sort of prostration which destroyed all notion of time.

I was startled when Gerda shouted loudly, slamming the front door behind her, "Not too serious. She's woken up. She'll recover. Not this time round!"

"Oh, good. A false alarm, was it?"

"Yes, the doctors will keep her under observation for a while, and then they'll send her back to me."

I looked at rustic Gerda, her shoulders as wide as her hips, her face splattered with freckles, her short arms.

"Are you very attached to your aunt?"

She shrugged her shoulders and said, as if it were self-evident, "The poor woman has no one else!"

At which point she turned on her heels and went to attack her saucepans.

The days that followed were fairly unpleasant. Getting news from Gerda about her aunt, who hadn't returned, was like trying to get water from a stone. And then, as if Emma Van A. could no longer protect the city with her weak body, Ostend succumbed to an onslaught of tourists.

The Easter holidays—I didn't know this—mark the beginning of the season in resorts in the North and as of Good Friday all the streets, stores, and beaches were teeming with visitors speaking all sorts of languages—English, German, Italian, Spanish, Turkish, French—with Dutch still predominant. Couples and families arrived in hordes, I had never seen so many baby strollers at once, enough to make you think it was a breeding farm; thousands of bodies were scattered all along the beach even though the thermometer did not rise above 17, and the wind continued to cool everything down. The men, who were hardier than the women, exposed their torsos to the pale sun; for them, it was more a question, when getting undressed, of showing their bravery than their beauty; they were taking part in a male competition that had nothing to do with women, yet they remained cautious, and kept their trousers or shorts on, as if courage extended only to their torso. For someone like me who had spent my summers on the shores of the Mediterranean, I was surprised to see only two colors of flesh: white, or red; brown seemed to be rare. In this northern populace, no one was sun tanned: it was either pallor or sunburn. Between livid and scarlet, only the young Turkish people displayed a caramel color, and not without a certain awkwardness. Consequently, they banded together.

Struggling to make my way through all the people, the dogs who were not allowed on the beach but who nevertheless tugged on their leashes toward the sand, the rented bicycles that hardly moved forward, and the pedal cars that were even slower, I suffered in this chaos as if it were an invasion. What right did I have, you may say, to use that word? What gave me the right to view others as barbarians when I had only preceded them by a few days? Did living at Emma Van A.'s house suffice to transform me into a native? It mattered little. I had the impression that by taking my landlady away, they had also taken my Ostend away.

And so I was truly happy when I heard the ambulance bringing her back to the Villa Circé.

The paramedics left her, in her wheelchair, in the hall, and while Gerda was conversing with her aunt, I had the impression that the old lady was fretting, as she glanced at me from time to time with a look that encouraged me to stay.

Once Gerda had gone into the kitchen to prepare the tea, Emma Van A. turned to me. Something in her had changed. She seemed determined. I went over to her.

"How did your stay in the clinic go?"

"Nothing in particular. Yes, the hardest thing was to listen to Gerda clacking her needles by my bedside. It's pathetic, no? Whenever she has a free moment, instead of picking up a book, Gerda embroiders, fiddles with some crochet, fusses with wool, that sort of thing. I hate it, women with their handiwork. Men, too, abominate such behavior. Take the North of Ireland, for example, the peasant women of the Aran Islands! Their husbands only come back to them—if they come back to them—with the wrecks of their ships, thrown up by the waves, eaten by salt, and the only way they can recognize them is from the stitches in their sweaters! That is what happens to women who knit: the only thing they attract is corpses! I must speak to you."

"Naturally, Madame. Would you prefer for me to take up residence elsewhere during your convalescence?"

"No. On the contrary. I insist that you stay because I would like to converse with you."

"With pleasure."

"Would you agree to join me for dinner? Gerda's cooking is no better than her coffee but I will ask her to make one of the two or three dishes she doesn't mess up."

"With pleasure. I am glad to see you are better."

"Oh, I am not better. This wretched heart will eventually give way. That is why I want to talk to you."

I waited for dinner impatiently. I had missed my dreamer more than I had realized, and I felt that she was in a confessional mood.

At eight o'clock that evening, once Gerda had straddled her bicycle to return home, no sooner had we begun our appetizers than Emma leaned over to me.

"Have you ever burned letters?"

"Yes."

"What did you feel?"

"I was furious that I had been obliged to do so."

Her eyes shining, she was encouraged by my response.

"Precisely. One day, thirty years ago, I too was obliged to toss into the fire all the words and photographs relating to the man I loved. I watched tangible traces of my fate disappearing in the flames; even though I was crying as I made that sacrifice, it did not touch me inside: I still had my memories, and always would; I told myself that no one, ever, could burn my memories."

She looked at me sadly.

"I was wrong. On Thursday, with this third attack, I discovered that my illness was in the process of burning my memories. And that death would finish off the job. And so: at the hospital I decided that I would speak to you. That I would tell you everything."

"Why me?"

"You write."

"You haven't read me."

"No, but you write."

"Would you like me to write what you are going to share with me?"

"Certainly not."

"And so?"

"You write . . . that means you are curious about other people. I just need a little bit of curiosity."

I smiled, and touched her hand.

"In that case, I'm your man."

She smiled in turn, embarrassed by my familiarity. After coughing to clear her throat, she smoothed the edge of her plate with her fingernail and, lowering her lids, began her story.

One morning, over fifty years ago, I woke up with the conviction that something important was going to happen to me. Was it a premonition or a memory? Was I receiving a message from the future or following a dream that I had partly forgotten? In any case, a murmur from the fates had used my sleep to leave this certainty within me: something was going to happen.

You know how stupid you become after insights such as this: you want to guess what is about to happen, and you distort it with your expectations. At breakfast, I fabricated several intrigues: my father was going to come back from Africa where he was staying; the mailman would bring me a letter from a publisher agreeing to publish my young woman's poems; I was going to see my best childhood friend again.

As the day progressed, all my illusions were destroyed. The mailman ignored me. No one rang at the door. And the ship coming from the Congo did not contain my father in its cargo.

In short, I found myself making fun of the enthusiasm I had had that morning, considering myself half insane. In the middle of the afternoon, almost resigned, I went for a walk along the shore with Bobby, the spaniel I had at the time; there too, in spite of everything, I found myself staring at the sea to make sure there wasn't some miracle taking place . . . Because of the wind, there were hardly any ships offshore, and no one on the beach.

I was making my way slowly, resolved to drown my disappointment in fatigue. My dog, who had understood that our stroll would be a long one, unearthed an old toy to play with me.

He began to bound toward the dune where I had thrown his missile, when suddenly he recoiled as if he had been stung, and began to bark.

I tried in vain to calm him down, checked beneath his pads to make sure he hadn't been stung by some insect, then I made fun of him openly, and went myself to pick up the ball.

A man came out of the bushes.

He was naked.

When he saw my consternation, with a strong hand he seized a clump of grasses and placed them in front of his sex.

"Young lady, please, don't be afraid."

Far from being afraid, I was thinking of something else altogether. The truth was that I found him so strong, so virile, so incredibly desirable that it took my breath away.

He held out his hand in entreaty, as if to reassure me regarding his intentions.

"Would you help me, please?"

I noticed that his arm was trembling.

"I've lost my clothing," he stuttered.

No, he was not trembling, he was shivering.

"Are you cold?" I asked.

"A bit."

The understatement was proof that he was well brought up. I was trying to think of a quick solution.

"Would you like me to go and get you some clothes?"

"Oh, please, yes . . ."

In the meantime I worked out how long it would take me.

"The problem is that I need two hours, one to go, one to come back; by then you'll be frozen. Particularly as the wind is picking up and night is about to fall."

Without further ado, I untied the cape I had been wearing as a coat.

"Listen, put this on and follow me. That's the best way."

"But . . . you'll get cold."

"Go on, I still have a shirt and a sweater, whereas you have nothing. In any case, I cannot possibly go along the beach with a naked man at my side. Either you take my cape, or you stay here."

"I'll wait here."

"You're so trusting," I said with a laugh, because I suddenly realized how comical the situation was. "What if, once I get home, I don't go back out?"

"You wouldn't do that!"

"How do you know? Has anyone ever told you how I ordinarily treat the naked men I find in the bushes?"

It was his turn to burst out laughing.

"All right. I'll take your cape, then, thank you."

I went up to him and draped the cloth around his shoulders, so he wouldn't risk revealing his sex on raising his hands.

Relieved, he wrapped himself up, although the woolen garment was not enough to cover his tall body.

"My name is Guillaume," he said, as if he considered it time for an introduction.

"Emma," I replied. "Let's not talk anymore, and let's go home as quickly as possible before the weather turns us into icebergs. Is that all right?"

We headed into the wind.

Once you assign a destination to your walking, there is no more unpleasant means of locomotion. Strolling aimlessly turns out to be a pleasure, but going from place to place seems interminable.

Fortunately, our strange couple did not run into anyone. As we were silent, I grew more and more intimidated by the minute, and hardly dared glance at my companion; I dreaded the wind might lift up the cloth and he might think my gaze was indiscreet. As a result, I made my way with effort, my shoulder blades were tense, my neck stiff.

Once we got back to the shelter of the Villa Circé, I wrapped him up in the afghan I had in the living room, rushed to the kitchen, and heated up some water. I was learning on the spot to be a good housewife, and I'm generally so clumsy and inept. While I was putting some cookies onto a plate, it occurred to me that I had just brought a stranger into my home on the very day when I did not have any servants about, but such petty mistrust annoyed me, and I returned briskly with my tray of steaming hot tea to the library.

He was waiting for me, smiling, shivering, curled up on the sofa.

"Thank you."

Now I could take a closer look at him. His face was smooth, his eyes light, his hair long, curly and golden; his lips were full, and his neck sloped tenderly to strong shoulder joints. One of his feet was sticking out from the afghan, and I noticed his leg was smooth, tapering, hairless, like a marble from antiquity. My living room was hosting a Greek statue, the Antinous idolized by the Emperor Hadrian, that splendid young man who, out of melancholy, threw himself into the blue waters of the Mediterranean; now this morning he had just reemerged, intact, from the green waves of the North Sea. It made me shiver.

He misinterpreted my reaction.

"You are frozen because of me!" he said. "I'm truly sorry."

"No, no, I'll get over it quickly. Here, I'm going to light a fire."

"Shall I help you?"

"Hands off! As long as you haven't yet found a way to wear those afghans tied around you without danger of immodesty, I advise you to sit still on the sofa."

I was usually very bad at getting a fire going, but now there were sparks, and very quickly violent flames were licking the logs while I poured the tea.

"I owe you an explanation," he said, savoring the first sip.

"You don't owe me anything and I despise explanations."

"What happened, according to you?"

"I don't know. I'll improvise: you were born this morning, you emerged from the waves."

"Or?"

"You were being transported on a cargo ship full of slaves on its way to the Americas, then the ship was attacked by pirates, and it sank in the harbor at Ostend, but, miraculously, you managed to slip out of your shackles to swim to shore."

"Why was I reduced to slavery?"

"A terrible misunderstanding. A judicial error."

"Oh, I see that you are on my side."

"Absolutely."

Cheered, he pointed to the thousands of books around us.

"Are you a reader?"

"Yes, I learned the alphabet a few years ago, and I've put it to good use."

"It's not the alphabet that gives you such an imagination . . ."

"I've been reproached so often for my imagination. As if it were a fault. What do you think?"

"In you, I find it adorable," he whispered, with a troubling smile.

As a result, I fell silent. My inspiration had left me, giving way to anxiety. What on earth was I up to, all alone in my house, with a stranger whom I had found naked among the bushes? Logically, I should have been afraid. And, deep inside, I did have the feeling that I was facing danger.

I tried to rationalize things somewhat.

"How long had you been on the look-out for someone, hiding in the dunes?"

"For hours. I had already collared two women out strolling, before you. They ran away before I could disclose anything. I frightened them."

"Your outfit, perhaps?"

"Yes, my outfit. And yet, it really was the simplest thing I could find."

We both laughed wholeheartedly.

"It was all my own fault," he continued. "I've been staying for a few weeks with my family not far from here, and this morning I felt the need to go for a swim. I left the car behind the dunes, in a place that would be easy to find again, and then because there was no one about, absolutely no one, I left my clothes under a stone and went for a long swim. When I came back to shore, I could find neither the stone, nor my clothes, nor the car."

"Blown away? Stolen?"

"I'm not sure that I came back to the same spot after my swim, because I only vaguely recognized things. What could look more like sand than sand?"

"And more like a rock than a rock?"

"Exactly! So that is why I did not suggest we look for my car behind the dunes, because I have no idea where it is."

"Absent-minded?"

"The desire to swim naked in the sea is irresistible. The call of the open ocean."

"I understand."

And it was true: I did understand him. I guessed that he must be a solitary soul, like myself, to feel such intense exaltation in nature. And yet, a doubt crossed my mind.

"You did intend to come back, did you not?"

"When I left, yes. When I was floating out there, no. I wanted it never to end."

He looked at me closely then added, slowly, "I'm not the suicidal type, if that's what you meant."

"It was."

"I flirt with danger, I seem to vibrate when I'm taking risks—probably some day I'll do something foolhardy, and that will be it, but I have no desire to die."

"So you have more of a desire to live?"

"That's right."

"And to run away . . ."

Touched by my comment, he pulled the afghan closer around him, as if to protect himself from my disturbing perspicacity.

"Who are you?" he asked.

"In your opinion?"

"My savior," he murmured with a smile.

"But what else? Let's see if you, too, have imagination."

"Oh, I fear all I possess is the alphabet, not imagination."

"What does it matter, who we are? You are just a magnificent living statue that I found on the beach, that I am thawing out, and that very soon I shall clothe, in order to restore it to its wife."

He frowned.

"Why are you talking about a wife? I'm not married."

"Excuse me, earlier on you mentioned . . ."

"My family. I'm staying here with my family. Parents, uncles, cousins."

What an idiot! I had only tossed out my comments about how magnificent he was because I assumed he was married, and

I was steaming with confusion, as if I were the immodest one now, standing naked before him. He looked at me closely, tilting his head to one side.

"And you . . . your husband isn't here?"

"No. Not at present."

He was hoping for a more detailed explanation. To give myself time to think, I hurried over to see to the fire . . . I was troubled to find how attracted I was to this man. I was in no hurry for him to leave; at the same time, I could not bring myself to tell him that I lived alone in this house. What if he were to take advantage . . . to take advantage to do what? I was not against the idea of him seducing me. Rob me? Judging by his outfit, he was more the type to be robbed than to rob. Molest me? He was not violent, no, that was unlikely.

Turning around, I questioned him abruptly: "Are you dangerous?"

"That depends . . . to fish, hare, pheasants: yes, because I go fishing and hunting. Other than that . . ."

"I despise hunters."

"Then you must despise me."

He was challenging me with a smile. I sat back down across from him.

"I'll make you change your mind . . ."

"We've only known each other for a few minutes, and already you want to change me?"

"We don't know each other at all."

He readjusted the afghan over his shoulders and continued in a low voice, "To answer your question, you have nothing to fear from me. I'm very grateful to you for having gotten me out of a tight spot, and for not hesitating to open your door to me. But I am taking up your time . . . Would it be possible for me to make a phone call for them to come and get me?"

"Of course. Would you like to take a bath first? Just so you can get warm . . ."

"I didn't dare ask."

We stood up.

"And if you have some clothes . . ."

"Clothes?"

"Yes, a shirt, a pair of pants, I'll send them back washed and ironed to you, naturally, I promise."

"It's just that . . . I don't have any men's clothes, here."

"And your husband's?"

"It's that . . . I don't have a husband."

Silence fell between us. He smiled. So did I. I collapsed into my armchair like a disarticulated puppet.

"I'm sorry I don't have a husband to help you out, but until now I had never realized that a husband might come in useful."

He laughed and sat back down on the sofa.

"And yet a husband can come in very useful."

"Oh, I can tell I'm not going to like what you're about to say! Anyway, go ahead . . . of what possible use could a husband be to me? Go on, tell me . . ."

"To keep you company."

"I have my books."

"To take you to the beach."

"I go with Bobby, my spaniel."

"To hold the door for you, stepping politely aside when you go in."

"I have no trouble with doors and I would not care for a husband who steps aside. No that's not enough, what else might he be good for?"

"To hold you in his arms, and caress your neck, and kiss you."

"Yes, that's already better. And then?"

"And then, he would take you into a bed and make you happy."

"Oh, really?"

"He would love you."

"Would he know how?"

"It must not be difficult to love you."

"Why?"

"Because you are an amiable person."

In a way that was as irresistible as it was unconscious, we had come closer to each other.

"Do I need to marry a man to get that? Would an admirer not fill the role just as well?"

"Yes," he conceded with a sigh.

Suddenly his face grew tense. He sat back abruptly, pulled a corner of cloth over him, stood back up, looked anxiously at the walls all around him then completely changed his voice and his tone.

"I am sorry, Mademoiselle, I am behaving badly with you. You are so charming that I have ignored the situation that has required your attention, and I have been taking inadmissible liberties. Forgive me, forget my attitude. Could you simply lead me to your bathroom?"

A newfound authority filled his voice; without hesitating, I obeyed him immediately.

Once he had gone into the bathtub, I promised him that some clothes would be waiting on the stool behind the door and I hurried to my room.

I rushed to open drawers and cupboards, and as I did so I ruminated over the scene. What had happened to me? I had behaved like an adventurer, I had flattered him, provoked him, excited him, yes, I had obliged him to court me . . . A desire to please had crept into me, spilling over into my words, making my gestures more fluid, my gaze heavier; in short, it had compelled me to transform all our conversation into flirtatiousness. In spite of myself, I had allowed an erotic tension to come between us. I had given the impression I was an easy woman, and I would have induced him to behave in too enterprising a way, had he not reacted at the last moment by reverting to his good education.

I despaired of the contents of my wardrobe. Not only could I find nothing that might be suitable for a man, there was nothing that was his size. Suddenly, the thought occurred to me to go upstairs to the maid's floor: Margit was tall, wide, podgy. I could take advantage of her absence to borrow something.

Bathed in sweat, I hurried away with the largest outfit in her trunk, and went back downstairs, shouting outside the door, "I'm ashamed, it's a disaster. All I can offer you is a bathrobe borrowed from my maid."

"It will be fine."

"You're just saying that because you haven't seen it. I'll wait for you downstairs."

When he came hurtling down the stairs dressed in this huge white cotton robe—collar and sleeves decorated with lace, if you please—we burst out laughing. He was scoffing at his own ridiculousness, I was giggling with embarrassment because this female garment made him seem all the more virile, in contrast, all the more powerful. I was daunted by the size of his feet and his hands.

"May I make a phone call?"

"Yes. The telephone is there."

"What should I tell the chauffeur?"

I was astonished that he was calling a chauffeur rather than a member of his family, and did not have time to understand his question, so my answer was completely off the mark: "Tell him that he is very welcome and there's also some tea for him."

Guillaume had to sit down on the stairs because my answer was making him shake with laughter. I was delighted to have this effect on him, although I didn't know why. When he had recovered, he explained, "No, what I meant was, what address should I give to the chauffeur so that he can find me?"

"Villa Circé, at 2 Rhododendron Street, Ostend."

In order to compensate for my ridiculousness and show him

that I was well brought up, I left him alone with the telephone and went into the kitchen where I noisily moved things around, the better to convince him that I wasn't spying on his conversation; I even added some humming as I banged the kettle, the spoons and the cups.

"You sound like the percussion section of a symphony orchestra when you make tea."

Startled, I found him on the threshold, looking at me.

"Were you able to get hold of your family? Are they reassured?"

"They weren't worried."

We went back to the living room with the teapot and some more cookies.

"Do you write, Emma?"

"Why do you ask? Everybody asks me that!"

"You're such a great reader."

"I've committed some dreadful poems to paper but I will go no further. Reading and writing have nothing to do with each other. Would I ask you if you are going to turn into a woman, just because you like women? Well, your question is just as absurd."

"That's true, but how do you know that I love women?"

I was silent. Trapped! Once again, in spite of myself, I had allowed my words to take a suggestive turn. Whenever this man stood less than ten feet from me, I could not help but try to charm him.

"I can just tell," I whispered, lowering my eyelids.

"Because I really don't have a reputation for it," he added in a low voice. "My brothers and cousins are far more the skirt-chasing type than I am. They reproach me for being well-behaved, far too well-behaved."

"Oh, really? Why are you so well-behaved?"

"No doubt because I'm saving myself for a woman. The right one. The true one."

Foolishly, at first I thought that this sentence was addressed to me. When I realized my mistake, my reaction was to try to head off in another direction.

"You aren't about to tell me that at your age, you haven't . . . you still . . ."

I did not finish my sentence, so dismayed was I with myself. Here I was, grilling an unbearably handsome man whom I had dressed up as a woman, to try to find out whether he was a virgin!

His jaw dropped, between stupefaction and amusement.

"No, to ease your mind . . . I have . . . had that experience. And a great pleasure it is, too. You must realize, in my circle there were many women older than myself, still superb, who delighted in initiating me at a fairly young age."

"You have reassured me," I sighed, as if he were talking about his prowess at golf.

"I do however prefer a good hike in nature, or a long ride, or swimming for several hours like this morning. I've prioritized my pleasures."

"I'm the same," I lied.

I used the excuse of a log that was about to go out to rush over to the fireplace.

"Why are you telling me this?" I grumbled haughtily.

"I beg your pardon?"

"Why are you talking to me about such personal things when we don't even know each other?"

He turned away, took time to think, then focused his eyes upon me, gravely.

"It seems obvious to me . . ."

"Not to me."

"We fancy each other, do we not?"

It was my turn to look away, to pretend to be thinking before training my gaze on him.

"Yes, you're right: it's obvious."

I think that at that moment—and for all the years that remained—the air around us changed for good.

The doorbell disturbed this harmony with its shrill ring. He winced: "My chauffeur . . ."

"Already?"

Life holds so many surprises in store: at noon I did not know this man, at twilight the idea of parting from him seemed intolerable.

"No, Guillaume, you can't leave like this."

"In a robe?"

"In a robe or in anything, you can't leave."

"I'll come back."

"Promise?"

"I swear."

He kissed my hand for an instant that was as rich as all my twenty-three years gone by.

As he was going out the door, I added, "I'm counting on you to find me again, because I don't even know who you are."

He screwed up his eyes.

"That's what is so marvelous: you didn't recognize me."

Then he closed the door.

I did not want to watch as he left; I was devastated, and stayed at the back of the dark hallway.

In a state of shock, I paid no attention to his last sentence; at night, however, as I went back over—more than once—every moment of our encounter, I wondered about these words: "You didn't recognize me." Had I already met him somewhere? No, a man with such a physique, I would have remembered. Had we been together somewhere as children? I wouldn't have recognized the child in the adult. Yes, that must be it, we must have known each other a long time ago, and then we grew up, he had recognized me, but I hadn't recognized him, and that is what his sentence meant.

Who was he?

I searched through my memories and could find no trace of Guillaume . . . this made me want him to come back all the sooner.

The next morning, he preceded his visit with a phone call asking for permission to come for tea.

When he appeared, he so impressed me with his elegant blazer, fine shirt, and classy shoes—a multitude of details that transformed the wild man into a man of the world. It was as if I was greeting a stranger.

He sensed that I felt awkward.

"Oh please, don't tell me you're sorry I'm wearing my own clothes. Otherwise, I'll put your maid's robe back on, I've brought it back."

He handed me a package wrapped in tissue paper.

"There is no point in threatening me," I answered, "I shall try to get used to you like that."

I led him into the living room where the tea and cookies had been set out. He seemed glad to be back in this décor.

"I haven't stopped thinking about you," he confessed, as he sat down.

"You've stolen the words from my mouth, that's exactly the first thing I wanted to say to you."

He placed a finger before his lips and said again in a quieter voice, "I haven't stopped thinking about you . . ."

"My love," I exclaimed, and began to sob.

I could not understand my reaction the moment this man was anywhere near me. Why had I burst into tears? To seek refuge in his arms—which was what happened the very next instant? No doubt . . . Visibly, another woman, far more feminine and clever than I, and who had been dormant inside my body, was aroused whenever he came near, and seemed to manage quite well: I let her continue.

After he had consoled me, he forced me to let go of him, and we sat down in separate armchairs. He asked me to serve the tea. He was acting rationally. Too much emotion can kill. This return to an everyday activity allowed me to regain my composure, and my strength.

"Guillaume, yesterday you recognized me, but I didn't recognize you."

His gaze was questioning, and he knitted his brow.

"Excuse me? I said I recognized you?"

"Yes, we used to play together when we were children, no?"

"Did we?"

"Don't you remember?"

"No, not at all."

"Then why did you reproach me for not recognizing you?"

He suddenly became very cheerful.

"You are truly adorable."

"What? What did I say?"

"You are the only woman who could become infatuated with a man who walks out of the sea. If I find it amusing that you didn't recognize me, it's because I am well-known."

"But do I know you?"

"No. But a lot of people do. Newspapers talk about me, and publish photographs."

"Why? What do you do?"

"What do I do?"

"Do you play some sport, or write, or win competitions? Car racing? Tennis? Sailing? That's the sort of talent that makes you famous. What do you do?"

"I don't do anything. I exist."

"You exist?"

"I exist."

"As what?"

"A prince."

This was so far from what I expected that I sat there dumbfounded.

He eventually grew concerned.

"Does this shock your beliefs?"

"Me?"

"You have every right to be of the opinion that the monarchy is a ludicrous and outdated system."

"Oh, no, no, no, it's not that. It's just that . . . I feel like a little girl . . . You know, the little girl infatuated with the prince. It's absurd! I feel ridiculous. Ridiculous that I didn't know who you were, ridiculous to have feelings for you. Ridiculous!"

"You are not ridiculous."

"If I were some shepherdess," I said, in an effort to act the clown, "that at least would make sense! The Prince and the shepherdess, no? However, I'm very sorry, I have no sheep, I have never kept any sheep, I fear I cannot even stand to be around them, they smell so dreadful! I'm a lost cause."

At least I seemed to be amusing him. He grabbed my hands to calm my feverishness.

"Don't ever change. If you had any idea how your ignorance delights me . . . Ordinarily, young girls swoon in my presence."

"Do be careful, I too am apt to swoon. I am sorely tempted, I confess."

The conversation continued pleasantly. He wanted to know everything about me, and I wanted to know everything about him, however, we were well aware that the purpose of our meeting was not to tell each other our past histories, but to invent a present for ourselves.

He came to see me every afternoon.

I must admit that it was thanks to him, and not to me, that we did not sleep together right away. I—or rather that very feminine woman inside me—would have offered myself already by the second visit. He insisted however that it should not happen too quickly. No doubt he wanted the moment to have its true value.

We went on meeting like this for several weeks, exchanging words and kisses. Until the day that it became unbearable for our lips to part.

Then I understood that, having proven his respect for me by preventing me from giving myself right away, he was now counting on me to give him a signal.

Which I did.

Emma Van A. interrupted her story. She cleared her throat and grew thoughtful.

"There is nothing uglier than a ragged old bag of bones talking about sensuality. I do not want to subject you to that. From the time one reaches a certain level of decrepitude, one ought not bring up certain topics, on pain of provoking disgust, despite one's belief it is concupiscence. Therefore, I shall go about it differently. May we leave the table?"

We went into the living room, among the books.

Adroitly, she maneuvered her armchair in front of the antique secretary, activated a mechanism that unlocked a secret drawer, and removed a delicate notebook of peach colored leather.

"Here. When I decided to become his lover, I put it down in writing."

"I feel terribly indiscreet . . ."

"No, no, please take it. Sit over there under the lamp, read it. That's the best way for me to continue my confession."

I opened the little book.

To my lord and future master
THE ALBUM OF LOVE
by Emma Van A.

As I find there is nothing more degrading in love than impro-vised, banal, or rough embraces, I am offering this menu to the man I fancy. As with any menu, he will use it, night after night, by pointing to what he would like.

1—The ordeal of Ulysses and the Sirens
Ulysses, you may recall, had himself bound to the mast of his ship to resist the hypnotic chanting of the sirens. My lord will be bound in like manner to a column, wearing as little clothing as possible, a blindfold to keep him from seeing, and a gag to keep him from speaking. The siren will walk around him, grazing him without touching him, and will murmur in his ear everything she wishes to inflict upon him. If the siren is gifted with imagination and my Lord is too, the scenes evoked will produce as great—or greater—an effect as if they had actually been performed.

2—The delights of Prometheus
Prometheus, punished by Zeus, was chained to a rock and subjected henceforth to the attacks of an eagle who came to devour his liver. I propose to chain my lord to something as solid as a rock but to devour something else. As often as he would like.

3—The visit in a dream
For the ancient Greeks, a dream was a visitation of the gods. My Lord shall be the dreamer, in the bed, stretched out naked on his back, and I shall persuade him that Aphrodite, the goddess of delights, has come to join him in his sleep. On condition that he does not open his eyes, or reach out his hand—in a word, does not move, except his hips, slightly, and I shall see to climbing onto him to perform the subtle movements that will bring us to a shared orgasm.
Variant: I shall be the dreamer and my lord the visitor.

4—The flute player
My lord will be the flute, and I shall be a musician. I shall play his instrument as a virtuoso. I am a good performer, and I hasten to point out that I play both the recorder and the flute. The first is taken into the mouth, the second caressed on the side.

5—The bear and the beehive
My lord will be a bear, running after the nectar of the flowers, while I shall be the beehive, unapproachable, as difficult to find as to reach. When the bear has found a position that makes contact feasible, I shall allow him to devour my honey with his inexhaustible tongue.

6—The original ball
Aristophanes has told us that in the beginning, man and woman formed a single body, a sphere that was then split in two, the male to one side, the female to the other. We will venture to re-create the original ball, holding each other close, fitting into each other in whatever way we can. The joints beneath the belly will require particular care. This will occur with a minimum of movement in order to refine the sensation and make it last. Nevertheless, the ball, like any sphere, has the right to roll on the bed or the carpets.

7—The disorientated ball
In this case, the ball must be put together by mistake, because not everyone has a talent for geometry. Thus, my lord's head might explore between my thighs while I shall have a look around between his. And while this is sure to fail, we shall try all the same to join together, using our lips to catch whatever we can find on the other's body.

8—The lighthouse keepers
There was a poet who claimed that love meant looking together in the same direction. That is what we shall try to do, like those who watch over dangerous reefs, with me in front, my lord behind.

9—The voyage of Tiresias
Some may recall this eminent Greek as a seer, others as the only individual to belong to both sexes, for the legend tells us that

he was male and female in succession. My lord and I shall under-
take to relive the experience of Tiresias: my lord will adopt the
attitude of a woman, and I shall adopt the attributes of a man.

10—Zucchini with melons
This is an old recipe from the Aegean Sea, which consists in
placing a zucchini between two melons to squeeze out the juice.

11—Waiting in the labyrinth
What is a labyrinth? A place where you get lost, one wall hiding
another, a deceptive way out, a mysterious neuralgic center that is
never reached. The game consists in multiplying the preliminary
approaches, like a prisoner in a labyrinth, going through the wrong
door, rubbing up against the wrong wall, tickling just next door—
in short, slowly reaching the point of extreme delight. It is not for-
bidden to find it, but it should be delayed as much as possible.

12—The Olympic Games
Like the athletes of antiquity, my lord and I shall be naked,
and covered in oil. We have two possibilities: struggle, or care. In
struggle, each of us shall try to place the other at his, or her, mercy.
In care, one will massage the other. The two activities are not
incompatible and may be practiced in succession. No hold is ruled
out, nor is any caress.

13—The snows of Parnassus
When Mount Parnassus is sprinkled with snow, the cold
leaves a burning memory upon the skin; and yet, the gods gath-
ered there. My lord and I, therefore, shall make love like gods,
with our flesh smarting not from snow, but blows.

I closed the volume, impressed. It would have been awkward to look at Emma Van A. right away, because I could not
imagine her writing such prose.

"What do you think?" she asked.

Just the question I did not want to hear! Luckily, I had no time to reply, because she took the text from my hands and said, "I won't tell you what he chose from the menu. In any event, right from the start, our embraces were astonishing. From the very first he was intoxicated with me, and I with him. I had not imagined it could be so enjoyable to spend my time with a man, who turned out to be lascivious, and sensual, always on the lookout for new pleasure . . . He liked nothing better than to come over to me and, his eyes shining, point to a line in this notebook. Who would go first? Did his desire arouse mine, or did he anticipate my intentions? I'll never know. The rest of the time, we talked about literature . . ."

She stroked the leather with the back of her hand.

"One day, he too gave me an identical album, with his menu set out just for me. Alas, later I was obliged to burn it."

She lingered in her memory, and left me at leisure to imagine, my mouth watering, what Guillaume must have written. What new whims? How far did he go, after his mistress's boldness? Beneath her sentences, her formality, these lovers from another era had given each other an unheard-of freedom, that of confessing their fantasies, and leading their partner into that place, refusing to allow their lovemaking to become bogged down by mechanical repetition, raising it to a moment of invention and erotic poetry.

"After he had read this notebook," continued Emma, "Guillaume was amazed to discover that he was the first man to possess me."

"I beg your pardon?"

"Yes, you heard me. He required proof in order to be convinced that I had been a virgin until him."

"I confess that these pages are nothing like the platitudes of an inexperienced virgin."

"I was a virgin but not inexperienced. Otherwise, how could

I have written these lines and then performed them! No, in Africa I was given a head start."

"In Africa?"

"That is what I explained to Guillaume."

I spent my childhood in Africa, in a large villa with columns, where servants tried to protect us from the heat by means of awnings and fans, but all they managed to provide was hot shade. I was born there, in the Congo, the jewel in imperial Belgium's crown. My father had gone to teach literature to the white bourgeoisie in Leopoldville, now called Kinshasa. He met a rich girl there in a society drawing room, fell in love and, although he had no fortune, only culture, he was able to win her hand. My arrival in the world was the cause of my mother's departure, for she died from complications after the birth; all I knew of her was a sepia photograph placed on the piano she used to play, now closed, imperial and silent, a photograph that faded too quickly: by my adolescence, all I could see of her was an elegant, chalky ghost. My father was the other ghost in my childhood: either he held it against me for having caused his wife's death, or else he despised me, for he was neither present nor attentive. My mother's dowry had made him rich, and he spent the money buying thousands of books in order to shut himself away in his library, which he only left to go out to give his lectures.

Naturally, like any child, I thought my everyday life was normal. If from time to time I envied my schoolmates because they had a mother, I did not consider myself unhappy, because I was surrounded by nurses with lilting voices, whose hips swayed as they walked, joyful servants who laced with pity the affection they felt for me. As for my father, his solitude and indifference only made him seem more fascinating. All my efforts in those days were toward a single goal: to grow closer to him, to be with him.

I decided I would cherish books as much as he did. In the beginning, as I read, I wondered what pleasure he could find in giving himself a headache to read such tiny black script—it is true that I had started with a treatise of Roman history in fifteen volumes—then by chance I came upon the novels of Alexandre Dumas, and was filled with enthusiasm for Athos, Aramis and d'Artagnan; from that moment, I became the reader I had initially only pretended to be. After a few years went by, when it had become clear to him that I was devouring thousands of pages every week, from time to time he would point to a spine, and say in a weary voice, "There, you should try that one." I would gratefully plunge into the text as if my father had said, "I love you."

When I was twelve years old, I noticed that from time to time my father, once he was sure I was in bed, would set off at twilight, an hour when he could no longer give any lectures. Where did he go? Where did he return from, an hour or two later, quiet, almost smiling, humming a tune now and again to his own amusement? I began to dream that he was courting a woman who would someday become my second mother.

I was not far from the truth: I would soon discover that he had unearthed an entire army of mothers! A battalion of women who became my friends . . . but I'm getting ahead of myself, let me explain.

One day, because he had stolen a flower from the bouquet in the dining room to put in the lapel of his new suit, I followed him, in secret. Imagine my stupefaction when I saw that he only went a hundred yards or so from our street, just round the corner, to the Villa Violette.

I begged the maids: who lives there? They burst out laughing, refused to reply, and then as I would not give up, they eventually described the place to me: it was a brothel.

Fortunately, Maupassant, one of my favorite authors, had taught me the existence of these establishments where women gave pleasure to men in exchange for money; better still, because he passed no moral judgment on the activity of prostitutes, and depicted them with so much humanity in *Boule de Suif* and *La Maison Tellier*, Maupassant had filled me with respect for them. Particularly as, in my opinion, they had been ennobled, even blessed, because they had inspired the pen of such a genius.

It was in that state of mind that I went up to the brothel of Madame Georges. What must she have thought, that fat red-headed woman with her gold teeth, squeezed into her made-to-measure dresses from thinner days, when she saw this little girl come up to her? I will never know. The fact remains that although I was initially discouraged by her chilly reception, over time I managed to convince her I was in good faith: no, I was not looking for work; no, I did not come to keep a jealous eye on my father; no, I would not write down the names of her clients in order to inform their spouses in Leopoldville.

"What you doing here again? What is it that attracts you? It's not very healthy for a girl your age to be so curious . . ."

"Indeed, Madame, I may be curious, but I don't see why it is unhealthy. I'm interested in pleasure. Isn't that what you offer here?"

"For money, that's what I offer, yes. However, there are other places where you can learn."

"Oh, yes? Where? There are no women in my house because my mother died; my nannies treat me like a little kid; no one wants to talk to me! I want to see women, real women. Like you and your girls."

Fortunately, Madame Georges loved to read novels. Since she no longer gave herself to men—or since they had stopped asking for her—she indulged in orgies of reading. By lending her the books she didn't have, and talking about them with her, I won her over, and in some confused part of her brain I was transformed into the daughter she would have liked to have. As for me, I played along with complete sincerity, for I was fascinated by Madame Georges, or rather by her world.

Because she ran a business that was devoted to men's pleasure, she was not afraid of them.

"Don't be afraid of men, my girl, they need us as much as we need them. There's no reason for you to keep quiet, ever. Remember that."

Over time, I was allowed access to the Blue Salon, a room where no males had the right to enter. That is where the girls rested between two clients, chatting together; as the weeks went by, they got used to me, and stopped paying attention to what they talked about, and I finally discovered what went on between men and women, from every angle, with every varia-tion. I learned about love the way a chef learns about gas-tronomy, by staying in the kitchen.

Out of friendship, one of them allowed me to use "Madame's trap door," an opening that was built into every room so that Madame could keep an eye on any suspicious clients.

So, between the age of twelve and seventeen, I was a fre-quent visitor to Madame Georges's brothel. It became a second home. As incredible as it may seem, there was so much tender-ness between us that Madame Georges kept my visits a secret. We were both intensely curious about other people, but she had satisfied her curiosity through prostitution, then reading. She insisted, moreover, that I must not imitate her, or any of her boarders, and she took charge of a part of my education.

"Your style has to be pure, with a 'healthy girl' aspect, a sort of eternal virgin, but modern. Even if you wear makeup, you have to give the impression you have nothing on your face."

So, while I spent my days in the company of whores, I looked as respectable as can be.

Then one day one of my cousins saw me go in and come out of the Villa Violette, and tattled on me to my father.

He called me into his solemn study, on the day I turned sev-enteen, to demand an explanation.

I told him everything, without hiding a thing.

"Swear to me, Emma, that, well, you understand, you never gave, anybody—"

He couldn't finish his sentence. I think that in the course of this conversation he was discovering that he was my father and, for the first time, that he had a duty toward me.

"Papa, I swear I didn't. And you know Madame Georges, she doesn't fool around! When she says something is a certain way, then that's the way it is."

"That's . . . that's true" he muttered, blushing, embarrassed that I was acquainted with this Madame Georges, who had had her share in organizing an existence he had hoped to keep secret.

I went on, specifying that I was neither ashamed of spending my time there, nor of having a Madam as my best friend, and you'd really have to be a dolt like my cousin not to grasp that.

"I see . . ." he conceded, to his own surprise.

Not only was he astonished to discover who I was, but he was astonished to find that he liked me, in the end. This discussion, which should have been stormy yet was not, marked the beginning of a new relationship between my father and me, our happy years . . . Until we left the Congo, that is how we lived, spending our time, both he and I, between two houses, our own and the Villa Violette.

"And that is how Guillaume found me, an experienced virgin, a woman who had given herself to no one but was not afraid, either of men, or their bodies, or sex. Health problems required me to go back to Belgium; once my treatment was over, I came to rest in this family house. My father wanted to join me here, and he settled in for six months, bringing home all his library, then he missed the Congo so much—or was it the Villa Violette?—that he went back there. Guillaume met me the year I turned twenty-three. In the beginning, our affair remained a secret. Out of caution, no doubt. And modesty, too.

The pleasure of clandestine meetings. And then, it seemed we got into the habit, and our affair remained clandestine. Outside his aide-de-camp, his secretaries, and his servants whom circumstances obliged us to trust, no word got out about our affair. We avoided any gossip, or photographers, we never appeared anywhere together in public. We hid here, apart from a few escapades abroad, in countries where Guillaume was an unknown tourist."

"Why?" I dared to interrupt her.

Emma Van A. hesitated, her jaw trembled, as it she was forcing herself to keep certain words inside. Her gaze swept the room, and it took her a moment to reply.

"I had chosen a man, not a prince. I had chosen to be a mistress, not a spouse, still less a lady-in-waiting, with the obligations that would imply."

"Did you refuse the idea of a marriage?"

"He didn't suggest it."

"Might you have been waiting for him to propose?"

"No, that would have proved that he hadn't understood anything, either about me, or about ourselves, or about his duties. And besides, let's be perfectly clear, dear sir, a royal heir, whatever his rank regarding accession to the throne, does not wed a woman who cannot have children."

That was the confession that cost her so dear. I looked at her compassionately. She went on, relieved, "We took no precautions where love was concerned. After five years, I gave up: my womb was as dry as the Gobi desert. I will never know, anyway, whether it was physiological, or whether the memory of my mother who died in childbirth had caused my womb to be barren."

"What happened?"

"In the beginning, nothing changed. Then he confessed that the royal family was giving him a hard time, and the press, too; it wasn't enough to see him practicing sports, they were beginning to doubt his virility. In these blue blooded lineages, there are a considerable number of homosexuals, so the true ladies' men are obliged to procreate in order to reassure the people and secure the monarchy. It was his destiny as a man and as a prince. He had tried to ignore it for as long as possible . . . I urged him to react."

"Which means?"

"To take mistresses, and be seen in public with them."

"Did you separate?"

"Not at all. We stayed together, and remained lovers, but he kept up appearances. He was allowed to have a few escapades, and each time they were so awkward and indiscreet that invariably there were photos in the newspapers."

"How could you stand it, knowing he was being unfaithful to you?"

"It was easy: I was the one who chose his mistresses."

"I beg your pardon?"

"You heard me perfectly well. I chose the women with whom he had his affairs."

"And he went along with this?"

"That was my condition. I would only share him if I could decide whom I was sharing him with. Because he was crazy about me, he consented."

"How did you choose his mistresses?"

"Always very beautiful."

"Indeed?"

"Very beautiful and very stupid. While there are not ten ways to go about being beautiful, there are a thousand ways to go about being stupid—stupid because you have no conversation, stupid because your conversation is boring, stupid because you're only interested in what excites women and not men, stupid because you think you're more intelligent than you are, stupid because you have a one track mind. My poor Guillaume, I signed him up for the grand tour of the country of stupid women!"

"I get the feeling you rather enjoyed it."

"Absolutely. Well, I was kind, I only pointed him in the direction of decorative ninnies; if I had wanted to be nasty, I could have set him up with women who were both stupid and ugly!"

"How did he take it?"

"Very well. He knew how to appreciate what was best about them, and to flee from what was worst. He left me quickly, but he always came back just as quickly."

"Would you swear that he wasn't angry with you?"

"We would talk about the ditzy doll of the season; as the ones I chose were always picturesque, he had something to tell me. Otherwise . . . I will have to admit we had a good laugh. It was cynical on my part but we were under a double pressure: on the one hand, society obliged us to hide; on the other hand, it forced him to prove that he was a ladies' man; we had found a solution. When we were alone together, nothing had changed, we adored each other just as much, if not more, because we went through these difficulties together."

"Weren't you ever jealous?"

"I wouldn't let myself show it."

"So, you did feel some jealousy!"

"Obviously. How many times was my brain filled with images of him with his women until I felt like saying I'd had enough?"

"To commit suicide?"

"No, to kill those women. I had dreams of murder. But in fact they destroyed themselves, through their stupidity. That much was lucky, they were such nincompoops. One time, only once, did I nearly make a mistake!"

She waved her hands, as if she were still struggling against the danger.

"That wretched Myriam, she nearly got me. I've never seen a woman who put so much energy into trying to seem brainless . . . Guillaume sneaked me into the palace, where I took part in his meals, hidden behind some drapery, in order to confirm my choice of ninny. In the beginning I chose that Myriam because she spouted one stupidity after another, like a veritable machine gun of nonsense, until the moment I noticed she never said anything but amusing stupidities, always funny, never off the mark, never boring: it gave me a chill, and I concluded that she had a sense of humor, which is no less than a sign of refinement. After that, I paid closer attention, and I noticed that she behaved in a certain way with each of the men she met: if a man was starchy, she would let slip something like, 'He's a funny sort of fellow,' with a relaxing familiarity; if he was vain, she would come out with flattering things about his so-called success; if he was crazy about hunting, she would listen tirelessly, as if the conqueror of the rabbits were a hero of several world wars; in short, she was an ace charmer who hid her game very well. At dessert, she went over to Guillaume and talked to him about sports, persuading him that she wanted to do a parachute jump. It wasn't true, but she was perfectly capable of trying her luck in order to fall into his arms, she was an adventurer after all! I forbade her from coming to the palace. A clever little bitch who played the airhead, all the better to manipulate her men . . . She's had a brilliant career since then, she's married one important gentleman after the other, and each time, what do you suppose, worse luck: they were all rich!"

"Did Guillaume get attached to any of those women?"

"No. You know, men are not demanding regarding the conversation they have before getting into bed, because they are ready to deserve their reward; after bed, however, a man of taste and culture becomes strict again, don't you think?"

I looked down, silenced by this unanswerable truth.

She wiped her hands on her knees, and smoothed the folds of her skirt.

"That period with the mistresses, it may have been tiring,

but it was rather thrilling, because it also allowed me to become an expert in the art of ending relationships. Obviously! It was I who suggested the words to say when he left them. I invented them, loads of them, all the phrases destined to ditch them, their mouths gaping, speechless. The break had to be clean, no mess, no trace, irrevocable, no suicides."

"And?"

"We're getting there."

Now I suspected we were about to deal with the darkest period of this story, the one that would relate its culmination. Emma Van A. could sense it, too.

"A glass of port?"

"With pleasure."

While she busied herself, it allowed us to take a breather before attacking the rest of the story. She savored the fortified wine, in no hurry to narrate the end, dismayed that we had reached it so soon.

Suddenly, she turned to me, her expression grave.

"And yet, I realized that we could no longer go back. Up to then, we had postponed the issue, gone around the obstacle, and yet now the time was coming where he would have to get married and have children. I would rather it was I who rejected him than see him leave me. Pride . . . I dreaded the moment where I would no longer be the object of his affections, but his mother. Yes, his mother . . . Who else pushes a man to take a wife and have children, when she would really rather keep him for herself?"

Her eyes grew moist. Several decades later, the same reluctance overwhelmed her.

"Oh, I was not ready to become Guillaume's mother! Not for a second—I loved him so much, so passionately. I became resolved therefore to act 'as if.'"

She swallowed. Telling me must be as painful as it had been to do it.

"One morning, I informed him that I had to take him back

to where I had found him several years earlier, in the dunes. He understood right away. He refused, he begged me to wait. He cried, dragging himself along the ground. I stood fast. We went to the place where he had first appeared to me, we spread some blankets in the sand, and there, despite the damp, dreary weather, we had our last embrace. And, for the first time, without resorting to our book of pleasures. It would be impossible to say whether it was enjoyable; it was savage, furious, disenchanted. Then I handed him a drink where I had placed a sleeping tablet.

"By his naked body, fast asleep, as similar to a sculpture as on the first day, I picked up his clothes, put them into my basket with the blankets, then I took out the Dictaphone that I had stolen from him.

"Above his long legs shivering with cold, my gaze wandering over his muscular rump, his tanned back, his hair curling over his long neck, I recorded my farewell message: 'Guillaume, it was I who chose your mistresses; it is you who will choose your wife. I want to leave you the right to decide on your own how much you will miss me. Either you will suffer so much from our separation that you will choose someone completely the opposite from me, to erase any trace of me, or you will want to make me a part of your future and you will choose a woman who resembles me. I don't know what will happen, my love, I just know I won't like it but that it's necessary. I beg you, we must not see each other under any circumstances. You must act as if Ostend were at the other end of the planet, inaccessible. Don't torture me with hope. I will never open my door to you again, I will hang up if you call me, I will tear up the letters you send me. We are going to have to suffer the way we burned, terribly, inordinately. I will keep nothing to remind me of you. This evening, I shall destroy everything. What does it matter, no one can take my memories. I love you, our separation changes none of that. Thanks to you my life has meaning. Farewell.' I dashed away. When I got to the house, I informed his aide-de-camp so that he would go to fetch him along the coast before nightfall, and then I threw our letters and photographs into the fire."

She grew thoughtful, then continued, "No, that's not entirely true. At the decisive moment, I refrained from throwing away his gloves. You see, he had such hands . . ."

Her gnarled old fingers caressed an absent hand.

"The next day, I sent one of the gloves to him, and put the other away in my drawer. A glove is like a memory. A glove keeps the shape of the body, the way memory keeps the shape of reality; a glove lives as far from flesh as memory does from vanished time. A glove is woven with nostalgia . . ."

She fell silent.

Her story had taken me so far away that I did not want to interrupt it with banal words.

We stayed like that for a moment, in the thickness of time, so small among all the books, in a darkness briefly yellowed by lamplight. Outside, a furious ocean was raging.

And then, I went over to her, took her hand, placed a kiss on it and murmured, "Thank you."

She smiled to me, terribly moving, like a dying woman asking, "I've had a beautiful life, haven't I?"

I went back up to my bedroom, luxuriating as I stretched out on the bed, where her story fed dreams so strong that in the morning, I almost wondered if I had slept.

At nine thirty, Gerda called to me from the corridor, insisting on serving me breakfast in bed. With a brisk gesture, she drew open the curtains, then set the tray among the quilts.

"Did my aunt tell you her life story, yesterday?"

"She did."

"And it took all evening?" Gerda guffawed.

I understood that it was curiosity that was making her behave in such a friendly way toward me.

"I'm sorry, Gerda. I swore I wouldn't repeat anything."

"What a pity."

"In any case, you would be wrong to imagine that your aunt is an old maid who has known nothing in her life."

"Oh, really? My poor aunt, and here's me who's always believed she'd never met the wolf, and that she'd die a virgin!"

"Well, that's not the case."

"Well, I'll be! How about that . . ."

"Why were you so sure of it?"

"Well, she's an invalid . . ."

"Wait a minute! The stroke that confined her to her wheel-chair, that only happened about five years ago . . ."

"No, I was referring to her disability. Aunt Emma was not immobilized before her attack but she couldn't get around any easier. Poor woman! She had tuberculosis of the bones, back in the days when they didn't have the medication they have today. It affected her hips. How old was she then? Twenty. That is why she left Africa: she came to the hospital here . . . To treat her, they laid her out on a wooden plank for a year and a half, in the sanatorium. When she moved into the Villa, in Ostend, at the age of twenty-three, she could no longer walk except with crutches. The children called her 'the cripple.' Children are so mean, so stupid and heartless! Because she was pretty, my aunt, very pretty in fact. And yet, who'd want a girl who hobbled around? She swayed from one hip to the other with the shortest step; it was frightening, mind. In the end, everyday life became easier after her attack, when she finally accepted the wheelchair. I ask you, try to get a twenty-three-year-old girl to sit in a wheel-chair . . . You have to say things as they are: what a pity! Well, so much the better if there was a fine lad who, someday, made the sacrifice to . . ."

Disgusted by the very idea, she shrugged her shoulders and went out.

Thoughtful, I tucked into my solid Flemish breakfast, then

had a quick shower and went down to join Emma Van A., who sat facing the day, a book on her lap, her gaze clinging to the clouds.

She blushed when she saw me. The reaction of a woman who has given of herself. I felt that I needed to reassure her.

"I spent a wonderful night, thinking back over your story."

"So much the better. I was sorry, after the fact, to have bored you with it."

"Why did you omit your disability?"

She grew tense. Her neck stiffened, and gained an inch in length.

"Because I don't live the life of an invalid, and I never have."

Suddenly she inspected me from under her lashes, wary, almost hostile.

"I see that my oaf of a niece has been filling you in . . ."

"She mentioned it by chance and it certainly wasn't to make fun of you; on the contrary, she spoke of your troubles with compassion."

"Compassion? I hate it when people look at me that way. Fortunately, the man of my life did not inflict his pity on me."

"He didn't talk to you about your handicap?"

"Yes, at one point when he was in a mood to get married, when he hoped to make our affair official . . . I was disoriented! I answered him that although the people might accept a commoner, they would reject an invalid. And so he told me the story of a French queen, Joanna the Lame. He even called me that for a few weeks. I had to make a huge effort to keep my sense of humor."

"Is that why you wanted your relationship to remain clandestine? Basically, he accepted your disability much better than you did . . ."

She shoved her neck against the back of her chair. Her eyes clouded over.

"It's possible."

Her voice broke. Her mouth quivered. I understood that another secret was waiting for me behind her lips.

"What's the matter?" I said gently.

"The tuberculosis was the actual cause of my sterility. Because of the infection in my bones and the treatment I received I could no longer use the side of my body. Otherwise, perhaps I would have had the courage to marry Guillaume."

She stared at me intensely and corrected herself: "How idiotic, sentences like that, 'otherwise,' or, 'if I hadn't been sick!'—tricks of the mind to suffer even more! My fate could not unfold 'otherwise.' One should never fall into these hypotheses, they are a deep source of pain where you splash about hopelessly. I have known one disgrace and one grace, I have no cause for complaint! The disgrace: my illness. The grace: that Guillaume loved me."

I smiled. She grew calmer.

"Madame, there is a question I hardly dare ask you."

"Go ahead. Dare to ask."

"Is Guillaume still alive?"

She took a deep breath and then stopped herself from answering. Swiveling on her chair, she went over to a low table, picked up a flat silver box, saw that there were no more cigarettes, and pushed it away, annoyed. In disgust, she grabbed an antique tortoiseshell cigarette holder and with a proud gesture, raised it to her mouth.

"Forgive me. I shall not answer your question, sir, because I do not want to give you too many clues that might identify the man I have talked about. Suffice to say that Guillaume was not called Guillaume, it is just a pseudonym that I gave him in my story. You will also notice that I did not mention his rank in the order of succession. And finally, you will remember that I gave you no indication whatsoever of which royal family is concerned."

"Excuse me? You did not mean the Belgian dynasty?"

"I didn't say that. It could just as easily be the royal house of Holland, Sweden, Denmark, or Great Britain."

"Or Spain," I shouted, exasperated.

"Or Spain!" she confirmed. "I told you my secret, not his."

My head was spinning. Naïve, I had swallowed down to the last detail everything she had told me the night before. This discovery that, despite her emotion, she had controlled her story, cast a different light upon her—calculating, crafty.

I wished her a good day and set off on my walk.

As I strolled, a strange thought wriggled between my temples, a thought that escaped me. In a fleeting way, a memory was working its way into my brain, like a word on the tip of the tongue. I had been baffled by what Gerda had told me, and then Emma herself, and I now went about with a sense of uneasiness I could not define. I stopped several times on the long deserted piers. I contemplated the waves: I felt land sick, and I had to sit down.

It was Tuesday, and the tourists had vanished, restoring my Ostend to me, intact and empty. However, I was suffocating.

Ordinarily, whenever I stayed by the ocean, I had the impression that the horizon receded as far as the eye could see; but here in the north the horizon rose up like a wall. I was not looking out at a sea on which one could escape, but a sea where one can go no further. This sea was not a call to departure—it raised up its ramparts. Is that why Emma Van A. had spent her life here, to remain prisoner in the exile of her memories?

I clung to the iron guardrail that ran along the pier. When I had left the villa, for a brief split second I had been stung by something—a sensation, a memory that had left a bitter taste in my mouth. What was it?

As I headed toward a café in order to get something to drink, the answer came to me, because the *brasserie* chairs suddenly conjured a sharp image: the madwoman of Saint-Germain!

Twenty years earlier, when I had just moved to Paris to begin my studies, I had met this strange creature one evening when my friends and I were waiting to go into the cinema.

"Mesdames, Messieurs, I'm going to perform a dance for you."

A tramp of a woman with flat hair of an indefinite color— some of it was yellow, some of it ash gray—stopped in front of the group of people getting ready to go into the theater, left her bundles under a doorway, then stood among us, keeping an eye on her bundles all the while.

"The music is Chopin!"

Humming in a reedy little voice, she jiggled on her ballet slippers, that must have been white once upon a time, her gestures hindered by the pink shawl sliding against her flowered dress, while her timid beret threatened to fall off. What was fascinating about her was the negligent way she performed her number: as if she wanted to have nothing to do with rhythm or tempo; she hummed the melody when she happened to think of it, provided she had enough breath left; as for her movements, she barely took more than a step at a time. She was like a little moppet of the age of four pretending to be a ballerina in front of a mirror. I got the impression that she knew this, and that she thought she was the only one who could do what she was doing. I could see a faint smile on her lips, reproaching us for being such ignorant connoisseurs. "I can perform anything, they don't even notice, they don't deserve any better."

"There! I've finished!"

She saluted us with a slow, noble curtsy, gathering around her a vast imaginary skirt that ended in an invisible train.

Those who regularly came across her gave a smattering of applause. Either out of pity, or cruelty, we began to give her an ovation, whistling, bawling, getting onlookers to join in the acclaim until the moment when, bathed in sweat, exhausted by the curtsies she had added to her choreography, she exclaimed shrilly, "Now don't go getting ideas, there won't be any encores!"

She then walked along in front of us, her red beret outstretched.

"For the dance, ladies and gentlemen. For the artiste, please. Thank you, in the name of art."

I often ran into her after that. One day she came close to the queue, teetering, her nose crimson, her gaze blurred: clearly she'd had too much to drink. She put down all her stuff and mumbled a few notes, wiggled her legs, just enough to realize she was incapable of finishing her haphazard ballet.

It made her furious. She gave us a dark look, up and down.

"Are you making fun of a poor old woman? But I wasn't always like this, I used to be very beautiful, yes, very beautiful, over there in my bags I have photographs. And then, I was supposed to marry King Baudouin, the King of the Belgians, because the Belgians they don't just have miserable little presidents like we do, they have real kings! Yessir, I was nearly the queen of the Belgians, you heard me! Queen of the Belgians, just because King Baudouin, when he was a young man, he was crazy about me. And I was crazy about him. Hear that? We were very happy. Very. And then there was that scheming woman, that . . . that . . ."

She spat several times on the ground, disgusted, in a rage, trembling with hatred.

"And then there was that Fabiola!"

Victorious, she had managed to say her rival's name. Pupils dilated with spite, eyebrows raised, she harangued us violently: "Fabiola, she stole him from me! Yes! Stole! When he was crazy about me. She didn't care, that Spanish hussy, no respect, she wanted to marry him, she bewitched him. He turned away from me. Poof, just like that, in the blink of an eye." She leaned against a wall, and tried to get her breath.

"Fabiola! It's not hard to speak several languages when

you're born with your ass in butter, and you've got maids from England, Germany, France, and America! Pshaw . . . I too could've spoken several languages if I hadn't been born in the gutter. Thief! Thief! She stole my Baudouin!"

At the end of her tether, the tramp took hold of herself, and looked at us as if she had suddenly discovered we were there. In a flash she made sure that her bags were still where she had left them, not far away, and then, limiting her performance to movements of her upper body, she hummed a vague tune, waved her arms and hands for twenty seconds, and then bowed abruptly.

"There we are!"

Then she began mumbling two speeches together between her teeth.

"For the dancer . . . scheming bitch . . . adventurer . . . thief . . . thank you, for the dance . . . that bitch Fabiola!"

So that was who my dreamer from Ostend was taking me back to, none other than the beggar woman who used to cart around her dozen or so plastic bags and whom the students at the Sorbonne used to call the madwoman of Saint-Germain, since every quartier in Paris has its own eccentric.

Was my landlady any better? In a flash, the improbability of her story struck me. An affair between an invalid and a prince! To have power over a rich, free man, going so far as to choose his mistresses for him! The beginning and the end on the beach, between the dunes, so impossibly romantic . . . It was all too surprising, far too artistic! It was no wonder there were no longer any material traces of their story: it had never happened.

I went back over her story in the light of my doubts. Her peach leather notebook containing the lovers' menu: did it not correspond to the best erotic texts, those written by women? Masterpieces of sensual audacity in literature: aren't they often the work of marginal eccentrics, spinsters who know they are not destined for motherhood, and who find fulfillment elsewhere?

When I went back to Emma's, there was a detail that acted like a key opening every door: above the glass canopy there was a silver and gold mosaic spelling the name of the place: Villa Circé! You could tell that the panel must have been added after the building was completed.

It was all becoming clear: Homer was her womb! Emma Van A. had been inspired by her favorite author to conceive her episodes. Her meeting with Guillaume, foretold by a premonitory dream, transposed the meeting between Ulysses and Nausicaa, the young woman discovering a naked man by the water's edge. She had called her villa "Circé" the better to identify herself with the enchantress in the Odyssey who worked her magic artifices on men. She hated knitting, weaving women, those Penelopes to whom Ulysses takes so long to return. As for the menu of erotic recipes, that too was inspired by ancient Greece. In short, she had made up her so-called memories with literary memories.

Either Emma had had a laugh at my expense, or she was an inveterate liar. In either case, it seemed obvious to me, given her disability—that she had tried to hide—that she had embroidered the truth.

I went through the door, determined to prove to her that I was no longer fooled. But when I saw her slim silhouette sitting in her wheelchair looking out at the bay, my irritation subsided.

A tender pity came over me. Gerda had been right when she said, "the poor woman," when speaking about her aunt. The unfortunate woman had not had to work for a living, but what must her life have been, with her body—surely a sweet one— so humiliated by disability? How could anyone hold it against her for using what was left—her imagination—to escape from her existence, to enrich it?

And what right had I, a novelist, to reproach her for her poetic improvisation?

I went up to her. She was startled, smiled, pointed to a chair.

I sat down across from her and questioned her.

"Why don't you write all of this down? It is so captivating. Write a book, use fake names, and call it a novel."

She looked at me as if she were talking with an infant.

"I am not a woman of letters."

"Who knows? You should try."

"I already know because I spend my time reading. There are enough impostors as it is . . ."

I grimaced, reacting to the word impostor, because it seemed revealing to me that she was using the word, when she had lied to me the day before: an admission of guilt, in a way.

She noticed my grimace and took me by the hand, kindly.

"No no, don't take it badly, I wasn't referring to you."

I was amused by her misunderstanding. She inferred that I had forgiven her.

"I am sure that you are an artist."

"You haven't read me."

"That's true!" she retorted, bursting out laughing, "but you are such a good listener."

"I listen the way a child does, I accept what people tell me. So, if you had made up those stories yesterday, I wouldn't realize."

She nodded, as if I were telling her a nursery rhyme. I ventured even further: "Every time we invent something, it's a confession, with every lie we are sharing a secret. If you were making fun of me yesterday, I would not hold it against you, I would thank you, because you chose me to tell your tale to, and you considered me worthy of your story, you opened your heart and your fantasies. What could be more singular than creativity? Can one give anything more precious? I would have been very privileged. The chosen one."

There was a shiver on her features that showed me she was beginning to understand. I hurriedly continued: "Yes, you've recognized me, I'm a sort of brother, a brother in falsehood, a brother who has chosen, like you, to open up by making up stories. Nowadays, great value is placed on sincerity in literature. What a joke! Sincerity can only be a quality in a report or some sort of legal testimony—and even then, it is more a matter of duty than quality. Constructing a story, the art of attracting a reader's interest, the gift of storytelling, the ability to see close up something that is far away, or to evoke without describing, the ability to give an illusion of reality—all of that has nothing to do with sincerity, and owes nothing to it. Moreover, stories that are driven not by reality but by fantasy—scenes one would like to experience, stifled desires, repeated urges—all mean more to me than any minor news story in the paper."

She opened her eyes wide, twisting her lips.

"You . . . you don't believe me?"

"Not for a moment, but it doesn't matter."

"What!"

"Thank you all the same."

Where did she find the strength to punch me so hard? She struck my chest and I fell backward.

"Imbecile!"

She was furious.

"Get out of here! Leave this room immediately! Get out! I don't want to see you anymore."

Alarmed by the shouting, Gerda rushed into the library.

"What's going on?"

Emma saw her niece and thought for a moment before she answered. In the meantime, the sturdy woman had located me, on the rug, and was hurrying over to help me to my feet.

"Well I never, Monsieur! You fell over! How'd you manage to do that? Did you trip on the rug?"

"Precisely, Gerda, he tripped on the rug. That's why I called you. Now I'd like to be left alone, I need to rest. Alone!"

Faced with such authority from a timid old lady, Gerda and I hardly knew what to say, so we beat a hasty retreat.

Once I had found refuge upstairs, I was filled with remorse

for having precipitated this crisis. I thought Emma was a liar, not that she was disturbed. Her reaction showed me that she believed in all her fabulations. Now, through my fault, she was suffering even more. What should I do?

Gerda came to join me on the pretext of serving me some tea, but in fact she wanted to get more information out of me regarding the scene she had just witnessed.

"What did you say to her? She was hopping mad!"

"I told her that I might not believe everything she had told me yesterday . . ."

"Oh, yes . . . I get it, and now . . ."

"I added politely that I adored her story, and that it didn't matter at all if she was making it up. And then she hit me!"

"Ouch!"

"I didn't know she had gone so far in her ravings. Totally unbalanced. I figured she must be a liar, or fond of making things up all the time, but I didn't think she would turn out to be . . ."

"Crazy?"

"Oh, that word is . . ."

"I am sorry, Monsieur, but you have to admit that aunt Emma is deranged. Do you think that the novels you write are true? No. So, that's what I'm telling you: my aunt is out to lunch. Hey, it's not the first time we've talked about it . . . Uncle Jan said the same thing already. And Aunt Éliette did, too!"

I fell silent. I found it unpleasant to acknowledge that this crude woman might be right; when common sense looks like a wild boar with an obtuse forehead, wearing yellow rubber gloves and a dress with giant flowers, and her vocabulary is poor, her syntax deficient, I am not attracted to common sense. Nevertheless, I had to share her diagnosis: Emma Van A. had left the real world behind, to go into a world of make believe, completely unaware of the journey undertaken.

Gerda went off to prepare dinner.

As for me, I was prevaricating. Should I leave things as they stood, or go to calm Emma down? I could not stand making her unhappy. It would be better to lie than to distress her.

At seven o'clock, once Gerda had left for the day, I went down to the living room.

In the fading daylight, in the middle of the library gradually overtaken by gloom, she sat in her usual place, her eyelids red. I slowly went up to her.

"Madame Van A . . ."

My words were lost in the silence of the room.

"May I sit down?"

The total absence of reaction gave me the impression that I had become voiceless, transparent. However, although she neither spoke nor looked at me, through the excessive contraction of her muscles and the fact that she had reduced her field of vision, I felt that she could perceive my presence and found it unpleasant.

I improvised a solution to get out of the crisis.

"Madame Van A., I am very sorry about what happened earlier, and I feel completely responsible. I cannot understand what came over me. It must be jealousy. Yes, without doubt. Your past is so fascinating that I needed to believe it was untrue, that you had invented it. You understand, it's difficult for ordinary people like myself to learn that such . . . extraordinary things can happen. Please accept my apologies. I have been furious with myself. I wanted to trample on your happiness by shouting out that it wasn't real. Do you hear me?"

She turned to me as, gradually, a victorious smile appeared on her face.

"Jealous? Really, jealous?"

"Yes. I defy anyone who listens to you not to die of a fit of pique, of envy . . ."

"I hadn't thought about it that way."

She studied me, sympathetically. I insisted, in order to regain her trust.

"No doubt that is why you never spoke about yourself: to avoid arousing any violent envy."

"No. What held me back was my promise. And then the idea that I might be taken for a madwoman."

"A madwoman . . . why would that be?"

"There are so many miserable people who lead such a boring lives that they will tell incredible tall tales and end up believing them. I understand them in a way."

The mystery of words . . . Like birds, they land on a branch, and the tree does not even realize. And so Emma Van A. had just described her own case without recognizing herself, as if it were an illness affecting only other people.

I felt she was calmer. As a result, I felt the same sense of peace.

And so I left Emma Van A., in silence.

The next morning, at half past eight, I was woken by Gerda's screams: she had just found her aunt dead in her bed.

Paramedics, doctors, sirens, policemen, doorbells, doors banging, movement, and noise—all came to confirm throughout the day what we had found when we went into her room: Emma Van A. had succumbed to a new heart attack.

Gerda behaved impeccably. Full of sorrow yet efficient, she took care of everything, including me: she asked if I wanted to curtail my stay—two weeks had been paid for in advance—or not. As I decided to stay, she thanked me, both for herself and for her aunt's sake, as if I were doing them a personal favor, when in fact I did not know where to go.

Emma Van A. was groomed, made up, and laid out on her bed, while we waited for her to be placed in her coffin.

I continued my strolls, which brought me a strange comfort. Today there was a sad dignity about the sea, veiled in tones of gray. I had come to Ostend to recover from a broken heart, and I had imagined a vague, gentle, nostalgic sort of place, a fog I might be able to curl up in. I had been mistaken. There was nothing vague about Ostend—no more than poetry is vague—and yet I had recovered. Emma Van A. had restored intense emotion to me, and in her odd way she had put me back on my feet.

I savored these final moments as a privilege where she still kept us, Gerda and myself, at the Villa Circé.

At five o'clock, her niece brought me my tea, grumbling.

"The notary called to say there is a specific clause regarding her funeral: there has to be an obituary in two Belgian daily newspapers, two Dutch ones, two Danish ones, and two English ones. Mad as a hatter!"

"Have you already taken care of it?"

"The notary has taken care of it."

"Who is going to inherit?"

"Me, as she promised me, that I already knew. And she requested a wake of three days, which is normal, and then the strangest thing: she wants to be buried with a glove."

I shuddered. She went on, rolling her eyes skyward, "Some glove that is in a mahogany box at the very back of her wardrobe."

As I knew what this was referring to, I didn't want to sully her aunt's memory by telling Gerda the wild story.

Gerda came back holding an open box in her outstretched hands, looking suspiciously at its contents.

"Is it a man's glove, is that it, yes?"

"Yes."

Her niece sat down and thought, a troublesome effort for her.

"So she might have known a man?"

"A man's glove indeed," I asserted gently.

She smiled at me, understanding my reasoning.

"Yes, I see."

"A chaste encounter during a ball. The rest, pure fantasy.

The perfect stranger from whom she confiscated this glove and who never realized . . . That is what I believe, Gerda."

"That's what I believe, too."

I looked up and took down a book that was in full view on the shelf.

"It's easy to see what sort of reading suggested her fairytale to her."

I opened an exquisite edition of Charles Perrault's fairy tales, then pointed to a chapter, "Cinderella. She leaves her slipper behind on leaving the ball. The Prince picks up the slipper and goes to look for his partner."

I picked up the glove.

"This is the prince's glove that represents Cinderella's slipper."

"My poor aunt. Not surprising that her love stories are no more than fairy tales. Reality was too hard for her, huh, too violent. Aunt Emma wasn't just an invalid, she was a misfit. She was never anything but a dreamer."

I nodded.

"That's enough making fun of her," she concluded, "so I'll respect her last wishes. Doesn't matter where it came from, this glove, I'll put it there with her."

"I'll come with you."

We went into the death chamber, with its impressive silence, and I must confess that because of this glove, because it was the prop of a dream, I was moved when I went to slip it between the old woman's fingers, against her heart, her heart that had only ever beaten in a dream.

On the third day of mourning, Gerda, her husband, her children, and I went to say farewell to Emma Van A., and then as we were waiting for the employees from the funeral parlor, we played a game of tarot.

When the doorbell rang, I shouted to Gerda, who had gone off into the kitchen, "Don't bother, I'll get it."

I was surprised when I found only one man on the doorstep.

"Good morning, are you alone?"

"Excuse me, Monsieur, is this indeed the home of Madame Emma Van A.?"

This question alerted me to the fact that I was mistaken as to the visitor's identity, all the more so as I could see the hearse moving with majestic slowness at the very end of the street.

"Forgive me, I thought you were one of the employees from the funeral parlor. No doubt you must know that Madame Emma Van A. has passed away?"

"Yes, Monsieur, that is why I have come."

Turning around, he saw that the undertakers were climbing out of their vehicle.

"I'm glad I made it in time. May I speak to you in private?"

He was an elegant man, wearing a tie and an impeccably cut dark suit, and he spoke with the tranquil authority of those who are used to brushing aside the obstacles before them. With no cause for mistrust, I led him into the living room.

"Look, Monsieur," he said in French, with almost no accent, "I won't beat around the bush. I have come here with a very unusual mission that I myself do not understand. Allow me to introduce myself: Edmond Willis."

He handed me a card with a crest that I did not have time to look at because he immediately continued in a hushed voice, "For five years, I have been Secretary General in post at the Royal Palace of *. When I took over my duties from my predecessor—who in turn had taken over from his predecessor, and so on all the way back through time—I received a most preposterous order. Perhaps with each new transmission of the order something has been eroded? Or was there a deliberate effort to muddle the information? Whatever the case may be, at present we no longer have any idea who, in the royal house, is behind this request . . . In any event, the instructions are perfectly clear: should the Secretary General of the Royal Palace learn of the demise of Madame Emma Van A., Villa Circé, 2 Rhododendron Street, Ostend, his mission is to take this glove and deposit it next to the body before the lady's coffin is closed."

And he handed me a white glove, the twin of the one that Emma, on her deathbed, was holding against her heart.

PERFECT CRIME

In a few minutes, if everything went well, she would kill her husband.

The winding path grew perilously narrow a hundred yards farther up the slope overlooking the valley. At that point on its flank, the mountain was no longer an expanse of slope, but turned into a steep cliff. The least little misstep could prove fatal. There was nothing for the clumsy individual to cling to, no trees, no bushes, no platform; all that emerged from the rocky wall were jagged boulders ready to tear a body to shreds.

Gabrielle slowed down to look all around. No one was climbing the path behind them, there were no hikers in the opposite valleys. No witnesses, therefore. Only a handful of sheep, five hundred yards to the south, were greedily filling the meadows, their heads bent to the grass they were grazing.

"Well, old girl, are you tired?"

She winced at the way her husband called her "old girl": precisely the sort of thing he shouldn't say if he wanted to save his skin.

He turned around, anxious to know why she had stopped.

"Hang on a bit longer. We can't stop here, it's too dangerous."

At the back of Gabrielle's mind, a voice was sniggering at each word the future dead man uttered. "Spot on, you know just what's coming, it's going to be dangerous! You may even be in danger of not surviving, *old man!*"

A blazing white sun weighed them down, imposing silence

upon the high mountain pastures, where not a breath of air brought relief; you might believe that the overheated star wanted to turn everything it touched, plants and humans alike, into a mineral substance, all life crushed.

Gabrielle caught up with her husband, grumbling.

"Go on, I'm okay."

"Are you sure, my dear?"

"If I said so."

Had he read her thoughts? Was she behaving differently, in spite of herself? Her one concern was to carry out her plan, so she endeavored to reassure him with a wide smile.

"In fact, I'm really glad to be back here again. I often came here with my father when I was a child."

"Wow," he whistled, as he gazed upon the panoramic view of the steep slopes, "don't you feel small here!"

Her inner voice shrieked, "And you're about to become even smaller."

They resumed their climb; he was leading, she followed.

Above all, she mustn't lose her nerve. Push him over without hesitating when the time came. Without warning. Avoid his gaze. Concentrate on the right movement. Do it properly, that was all that mattered. As for her decision, Gabrielle had made it a long time ago, and she wouldn't go back on it.

He was beginning to enter the dangerous bend. Gabrielle was walking faster, but he didn't notice. Tense, hurried, her breathing hampered by the need to remain discreet, she almost slipped on a loose stone. "Oh no," exclaimed the voice, "you're not going to have an accident when the solution is so near!" Her moment of weakness gave her a gigantic burst of energy: she rushed up, and with all her strength she slammed her fist into the small of his back.

Her husband arched his back, and lost his balance. She gave him the *coup de grâce,* kicking him in both calves.

His body slipped from the path and began to fall into the

void. Frightened, Gabrielle flattened herself against the slope with her shoulder to keep from falling and to avoid seeing what she had just caused to happen.

It was enough just to hear it . . .

A cry rang out, already far away, filled with a terrible fear, then there was a thud, and another, while his throat screamed with pain, then more sounds of something hitting and breaking and tearing, and stones rolling, and then suddenly, complete silence.

There! She'd done it. She was free.

All around her, the Alps displayed their grandiose, kindly landscape. A bird was gliding, motionless, above the valley, hanging in a pure, cleansed sky. There was no shrieking of sirens to accuse her, no policeman rushing up waving his handcuffs. Nature greeted her—sovereign, serene, an understanding accomplice.

Gabrielle stepped forward from the slope and peered over the edge of the precipice. Several seconds went by until she was able to see the disjointed body that was not where she had expected it to be. It was all over. Gab had stopped breathing. Everything was simple. She felt no guilt, just relief. And already she no longer felt any connection with the corpse lying down there . . .

She sat down and picked a pale blue flower and chewed on the stem. Now she would have the time to be lazy, to meditate; she would no longer be obsessed by what Gab was doing or hiding from her. She would be reborn.

How many minutes did she stay like that?

The sound of a bell, although it was muffled by distance, roused her from her ecstasy. Sheep. Ah, yes, she would have to go back down, put on an act, sound the alarm. Damned Gab! No sooner had he left her than she still had to devote time to him, make an effort for him, make sacrifices for him. Would he ever leave her alone?

She sat up, serene, proud of herself. She had done the main thing, and now all that was left was to move a little further to find her reward: peace.

Going back the way she had come, she went back over the scenario. How odd it was to remember it, a plan she had come up with in a different time, a time when Gab's presence was still a burden to her. Another time. A time that was already far behind her.

She walked lightly, more quickly than she normally should have, because if she were out of breath it would help convince people that she was upset. She would have to suppress her euphoria, mask her joy at seeing these three years of fury disappear behind her, three years of sharp, stinging indignation planting its arrows inside her brain. He could no longer dish out any "old girl" remarks, no longer inflict his pitiful gaze on her as he held out his hand, no longer claim they were happy when it wasn't true. He was dead. Hallelujah. Long live freedom!

After walking for two hours, she saw some hikers and ran in their direction.

"Please help me! My husband! Help me, please!"

Everything went marvelously. She fell to the ground as she drew near them, hurt herself, burst into tears and told them about the accident.

Her first spectators took the bait and swallowed it hook, line and sinker, both her story and her sorrow. Their group split in two: the women went with her down into the valley while the men went off to look for Gab.

At the hotel Bellevue, someone must have informed the personnel ahead of time by phone, because they were all waiting for her with the appropriate expression on their faces. A gendarme with a pale face informed her that a helicopter was already on its way with a rescue team to the scene of the accident.

At the words "rescue team," she shivered. Did they expect to find him alive? Might Gab have survived his fall? She recalled his cries, and then how they stopped, and the silence, and she had a doubt.

"Do you . . . do you think he might be alive?"

"That is what we hope, Madame. Was he in good physical condition?"

"Excellent, but he fell over several hundred yards, bouncing on the rocks."

"We have already encountered more astonishing cases. As long as we don't know, it is our duty to remain optimistic, dear Madame."

Impossible! Either she was crazy, or he was. Was he saying this because he had information, or was he mouthing some stereotyped formula? No doubt the latter . . . Gab could not possibly have survived. And even if, through some miracle, he had survived, he must be broken, traumatized, crippled with internal and external bleeding, incapable of speech! After all, if it wasn't already the case, he would die in the hours that followed. Would he have time to mutter something to the stretcher bearers? Just before they winched him up into the helicopter? Would he denounce her? Unlikely. What had he understood? Nothing. No, no, no, a thousand times no.

She grasped her head between her hands and as she stifled her tears the witnesses thought she was praying; in reality, she was cursing the gendarme. Although she was sure she was right, that nincompoop had filled her with doubts. And now she was trembling with fear!

Suddenly a hand was laid on her shoulder. She jumped.

The head of the rescue team was staring at her looking like a scolded cocker spaniel.

"You must be brave, Madame."

"How is he?" cried Gabrielle, torn with anxiety.

"He is dead, Madame."

Gabrielle let out a cry. Ten people ran over to comfort her, console her. Shamelessly, she screamed and sobbed, determined to purge herself of her emotions: phew, he didn't make it, he wouldn't say anything, the resident fool had given her the willies for nothing.

All around, everyone was feeling sorry for her. What exquisite delight, to be a murderer yet be taken for the victim . . . She indulged in it until the evening meal which, naturally, she refused to eat.

At nine o'clock, the police came back to inform her that they had to question her. Although she acted surprised, she had been expecting it. Before carrying out her plan, she had rehearsed her testimony, which had to be persuasive regarding the premise of an accident, and refute any of the suspicion that typically might fall upon the spouse when a partner dies.

They took her to the pink stucco police station, where she gave her version of the events while gazing at a calendar with a picture of three adorable kittens.

Although the policemen apologized for burdening her with this or that question, she went on as if she could not for a second imagine being suspected of anything. She cajoled them, signed the statement, and went back to the hotel to spend a peaceful night.

The next morning, her son and two daughters arrived, accompanied by their spouses, and this time the situation was awkward. She felt genuine remorse when faced with her beloved children's sorrow; it wasn't regret over having killed Gab, but shame at inflicting this pain upon them. What a pity he had also been their father! How stupid of her not to have conceived them with another man, to spare them these tears for him . . . In any case, it was too late. She took refuge in a sort of vacant speechlessness.

The only practical advantage of their presence was that, in order to spare their mother, they went to identify the body in the morgue. Which she appreciated.

They also tried to intercept any articles in the regional press reporting the tragic fall, scarcely imagining that the titles "Accidental Hiking Death," or "Victim of his own lack of caution," were a boon to Gabrielle, because they confirmed, in black and white, that Gab had died and she was innocent.

There was one detail however, that displeased her: when she got back from the coroner's office her eldest daughter, eyes red, felt obliged to whisper in her mother's ear: "You know, even dead, Papa was very handsome." What on earth was she on about, that kid? Whether Gab was handsome or not, that was no business of anyone's but Gabrielle, and Gabrielle alone! Hadn't she already suffered enough because of it?

After that remark, Gabrielle kept herself to herself until the funeral was over.

When she went back to her house in Senlis, neighbors and friends came to offer their condolences. While she greeted her neighbors with pleasure, she quickly became exasperated with having to tell the same story over and over only to hear them echo identical platitudes. Behind her sad, resigned expression, she was boiling with anger: what good was it getting rid of her husband if she had to talk about him all the time! All the more so that she was impatient to run up to the third floor, knock down the wall, ransack his hiding place and uncover the very thing that was tormenting her. Couldn't they just hurry up and leave her alone!

Their private mansion, very nearly a fortified château, was like something out of a book of fairytales, for under the tangle of climbing roses there were a multitude of turrets, crenella-tions, arrow slits, sculpted balconies, decorative rosettes, sweeping staircases, windows with gothic points and colored panes. With experience, Gabrielle increasingly relied on her visitors' exclamations to determine how little culture they might have, and she had classified them into four categories, from the barbarian to the bore. The barbarian would give a hostile glance at her walls and grumble, "Kind of old, here"; the bar-barian who thought he had some culture would murmur, "This is medieval, is it not?"; the truly cultured barbarian would detect the illusion: "Medieval style, but built in the 19th century?"; and finally the bore would cry out, "Viollet-le-Duc!" before boring everybody with a running commentary on each element that the famous architect and his workshop might have deformed, restored, or invented.

There was nothing surprising about a residence like this in Senlis, a village in the Oise, to the north of Paris, which featured many such historical dwellings on its hillside. Alongside stones dating from the time of Joan of Arc or buildings erected in the 17th and 18th centuries, Gabrielle's home seemed, in fact, to be one of the least elegant, for it was recent—a century and a half—and its taste was debatable. Nevertheless, she had lived there as one half of a couple from the time she had inherited it from her father, and she found it very amusing that her walls denounced her as a nouveau riche, for she had never considered herself to be either rich or newly so.

On the third level of the dwelling, which would have enchanted Alexandre Dumas and Sir Walter Scott, there was a room that belonged to Gab. After their wedding, in order to make him feel well and truly at home when he moved into her house, they had agreed that he would have the total use of that part and Gabrielle would have no say in the matter; she had permission to go and fetch him there should he be late for any reason, but otherwise she was not to go there.

There was nothing exceptional about the place—books, pipes, maps, globes—and it offered only minimal comfort in the form of torn leather armchairs, but there was an opening in the thick wall, obstructed by a vertical trap door. Gab had made room for it twenty years earlier when removing some bricks. Whenever he put something in there, he would cover the surface over again with roughcast in order to hide the recess from view. Because of his precautions, Gabrielle knew that she could not be indiscreet without providing proof of it. Out of love initially, then out of fear, she had always respected Gab's secret. Often, he made fun of it, and joked about it, testing her resistance . . .

Now there was nothing stopping her from breaking through the plaster wall.

The first three days, she thought it would seem indecent to go up there with a hammer and wrecking bar; and in any case, given the stream of visitors, she wouldn't have had time. On the fourth day, when she saw that neither the telephone nor the doorbell were ringing, she promised herself that after a quick visit to her antique store, three hundred yards down the road, she would satisfy her curiosity.

At the very edge of town, the sign "G. and G. de Sarlat" in golden letters soberly announced an antique store of the kind that the region preferred: a place where one could hunt around both for major items—dressers, tables, wardrobes—to furnish immense secondary residences, and for knickknacks—lamps, mirrors, statuettes—to decorate well-furnished interiors. There was no particular style that dominated there, but most were represented, including some dreadful imitations, provided they were over a hundred years old.

Gabrielle's two employees brought her up to date regarding the items sold during the fateful vacation in Savoie, then she spoke to her bookkeeper. After a brief meeting, she walked through the store that had filled with gossipy women the moment they had heard in the immediate neighborhood that "poor Madame Sarlat" was in her boutique.

She shuddered on seeing Paulette among them.

"My poor sweetheart," exclaimed Paulette, "so young and already a widow!"

Paulette looked for an ashtray to put down her cigarette, smeared with orange lipstick, but could not find one, so she stubbed it out under her green heel, visibly unconcerned that she might burn the linoleum, and came toward Gabrielle, spreading her arms dramatically.

"My poor dear, I am so unhappy to see you unhappy."

Gabrielle submitted to her embrace, trembling.

Paulette remained the only woman that she dreaded, for she was very gifted at ferreting out the truth in other people. Many considered her to be the most spiteful gossip, and she had the gift of penetrating people's skulls with a laser beam—her insistent gaze, her protruding eyes—and then to find the turn of phrase that could demolish an individual's reputation forever.

In the time it took to submit to her embrace, Gabrielle nearly choked on a few strands of Paulette's dry, yellow hair, exhausted by decades of styling and hair dye, then she bravely confronted the face shining with swarthy foundation cream.

"Say, did the police question you? They must have asked you if you killed him, right?"

That's it, thought Gabrielle, she already suspects me. She doesn't waste her time, she goes straight for the jugular.

Gabrielle nodded, bending her head. Paulette reacted with a scream, "Bastards! To make you go through that! Someone like you, so crazy about your Gab, for thirty years you ate the carpet in his presence! Someone like you who'd have had any operation he asked for, who'd have changed into a mouse or a man! I'm not surprised! Bastards! They're all bastards! Do you know what they did to me? When I was bringing up my second boy, Romuald, one day I had to take him to the hospital because the kid was all black and blue from slipping on getting out of the tub, can you imagine, the police came to get me at the emergency room to ask me if I hadn't been battering him! Yes! They dragged me down to the station. And locked me up. Me! It lasted for forty-eight hours. Me, their mother, they thought I was guilty when all I'd done was drive my kid to the hospital. Swine! And did they do the same to you?"

Gabrielle understood that Paulette, far from suspecting her, was taking her side. She was sympathizing, as a former victim herself. For her, any woman who was interrogated by the police would logically become, by analogy with her own case, an innocent victim.

"Yes, me too, that very evening."

"Jackals! How long?"

"Several hours."

"Scumbags! My poor chick, was it humiliating, then?"

Paulette, offering Gabrielle the tenderness she felt for her own self, again crushed her friend against her chest.

Relieved, Gabrielle allowed her to rant and rave for a moment, then she went home to get started on Gab's hiding place.

At noon, she went up the steps, the tools in her hand, and began to destroy the protective covering. The board jumped out, revealing a space where four small chests had been piled up.

She pulled over a low table and put the chests on it. While she had no idea what they contained, she did recognize them, for they were big metal cookie tins, and although the labels had been eroded by time and damp, you could still read "Madeleines from Commercy," "Mint Humbugs," "Lyon Marzipan Pillows," and other such sweets.

She was about to lift the first lid when the doorbell rang.

Leaving aside her labors, she closed the door behind her with the key in the lock, then went down to open the door, determined to get rid of the importunating bore without delay.

"Police, Madame! May we come in?"

Several strong-jawed men were standing on the threshold.

"Of course. What do you want?"

"Are you Gabrielle de Sarlat, the wife of the late Gabriel de Sarlat?"

"Yes."

"Come with us, please."

"Why?"

"You are wanted at the police station."

"If it's to answer questions about my husband's accident, your colleagues in Savoie already took care of that."

"This is an entirely different matter, Madame. You are suspected of having killed your husband. A shepherd claims he saw you push him over the edge."

After ten hours in police custody, Gabrielle was hesitant to confirm whom she despised more, the police chief or her lawyer. Perhaps she might have forgiven the police chief . . . When he was tormenting her, he was merely doing his job, adding neither viciousness nor passion, he was honestly trying to transform her into a culprit. Her lawyer, on the other hand, disturbed her because he wanted to know. And yet she was paying him to believe, not to know! What she was buying was his knowledge of the law, his experience of the courtroom, his energy to defend her; she didn't care one way or the other whether he knew the truth.

The moment they were alone together, Maître Plissier, a good-looking, dark-haired man of forty, leaned toward his client with a self-important air and in a grave voice, the kind of voice given to heroic cowboys in dubbed American Westerns, he said: "Now, I would like you to tell me, and only me, the truth, Madame Sarlat. It will not leave these walls. Did you push your husband?"

"Why would I do such a thing?"

"Do not answer me with a question. Did you push him?"

"That was my answer: 'Why would I do such a thing?' I have been accused of a senseless act. I loved my husband. We were happy together for thirty years. We had three children together, who can testify to that."

"We can plead a crime of passion."

"A crime of passion? At the age of fifty-eight? After thirty years of marriage?"

"Why not?"

"At the age of fifty-eight, Monsieur, if we are still in love, it's because we like one another, in a lucid sort of way, a harmonious, dispassionate affair, without excess, without drama."

"Madame Sarlat, stop telling me what I am to think but tell me rather what you think. You might have been jealous."

"Ridiculous!"

"Was he cheating on you?"

"Don't defile him."

"Who stands to inherit from your husband?"

"Nobody, he had no possessions. All the capital belongs to me. Moreover, we were married under separation of property."

"And yet, his last name is that of a good family . . ."

"Yes, Gabriel de Sarlat, people are always impressed. They think I married a fortune whereas I only married a name with a handle. My husband didn't have a penny to his name, and he never knew how to make money. Our property comes from me, from my father, rather, Paul Chapelier, the orchestra conductor. My husband's disappearance does not improve my financial situation; it changes nothing, it even makes it worse, because he was the one who used to transport the antiques that we sold in the shop in his van and if I want to continue, I will have to hire an extra employee."

"You didn't answer my question."

"I've done nothing but, Monsieur."

"Maître . . ."

"Don't be ridiculous. There is nothing I stand to gain through my husband's death. Perhaps he would have gained more from mine."

"Is he the one then, who tried to push you, with that very intention?"

"Are you mad?"

"Think about it. We could support such a hypothesis, that there was a struggle. On that mountain path, he decided to get rid of you in order to have your money. By pushing him, you merely resorted to self-defense."

"Separation of property! He would not have inherited a

thing upon my death, nor would I upon his. And why are you making up such improbable scenarios?"

"Because a man saw you, Madame! The shepherd tending his flock says that you rushed up to your husband and pushed him into the void."

"He is lying!"

"Why should he lie, what purpose would that serve?"

"It's absolutely extraordinary. When I suggest that there is no reason for me to kill my husband, whom I love, you doubt me, whereas you believe the shepherd on the pretext that there is no reason for him to lie! It's a double standard! Who hired you? The shepherd, or me? It's unbelievable! I can give you a hundred reasons why your shepherd might be lying: to look interesting, to become the hero of his canton, to take revenge on a woman or several women through me, to stir up shit just for the pleasure of stirring up shit! And besides, how far away was he? Five hundred yards? Eight hundred yards? A mile?"

"Madame de Sarlat, don't go making up my defense for me. The shepherd's testimony against us is damning: he saw you!"

"Well, I didn't see him."

Maître Plissier paused to look closely at Gabrielle. He sat down next to her and ran his hand over his forehead, worried.

"Am I to take that for a confession?"

"What?"

"You looked all around before you pushed your husband and you didn't notice anyone. Is that what you are confessing to me?"

"Monsieur, I am trying to make it clear to you that after my husband's fall, I looked all around and shouted out, loudly, because I was looking for help. Your famous shepherd did not come forward, did not reply. That's rather odd, don't you think? If he had gone to alert the guides, or down to where my husband was lying, perhaps then . . . If he's accusing me, isn't it to protect himself?"

"From what?"

"Non-assistance to a person in danger. I am talking about my husband. And about myself, by extension."

"That's not a bad idea to turn the situation around, however, I have to be the one to put forward such an argument. Coming from you it would sound fishy."

"Oh, really? You can accuse me of something monstrous, but I mustn't seem too clever, how pleasant!"

She pretended to be irritated although basically she was glad she had understood how to manipulate her lawyer.

"I'll drag him in front of the courts, that shepherd, see if I don't!"

"For the time being, you're the one who has been indicted, Madame."

"I had to go tearing down the mountain for hours to find some hikers and alert the rescuers. Your shepherd, if he saw my husband fall, why didn't he go to help him? Why didn't he alert anyone? Because if he had reacted quickly, perhaps my husband would still be alive . . ."

Then, exasperated at having to do the lawyer's job for him, she decided to have a crying fit and she sobbed for a good ten minutes.

Once her convulsion was over, Maître Plissier, who had been duly moved, began henceforth to believe everything she said. She scorned him all the more for his reversal of attitude: to let himself be worn down by a few sobs, what an oaf! Basically, when faced with a woman full of resolve, there was not a man on earth any smarter than the next one.

The chief of police came back and began his interrogation. He kept going over the same points; Gabrielle replied in identical fashion, although not as sharply as with her lawyer.

As the police chief was cleverer than the lawyer, after he had excluded any motives of interest, he went back to the relationship between Gabrielle and Gab.

"Be frank with me, Madame Sarlat, did your husband not want to leave you? Did he have a mistress? Or mistresses? Was your relation as satisfying as before? Did you have any reason to reproach him?"

Gabrielle understood that her fate would be determined by this gray zone, and she adopted a tactic that she would maintain to the end.

"I'm going to tell you the truth, officer: Gab and I were the luckiest couple in the world. He never cheated on me. I never cheated on him. Try to find someone to tell you the contrary: you won't. Not only did I love my husband more than anything in the world, but I shall never get over his death."

If at that moment Gabrielle had known where a few months later this defense tactic would lead her, perhaps she would not have been so proud of her idea . . .

Two and a half years.

Gabrielle was remanded in custody for two years while waiting for her trial.

Several times her children tried to obtain parole for her, arguing that she should be presumed innocent, but the judge refused for two reasons: one essential one, the other contingent: the first was the shepherd's testimony for the prosecution, the second the controversy that was exacerbated in the newspapers implying that judges were too lenient.

Despite the hard life in prison, Gabrielle did not get depressed. Just as she had waited to be liberated from her husband, now she was waiting to be liberated from this accusation. She had always been patient—a necessary quality when you work in the antique business—and she refused to be discouraged by this unexpected turn of events.

In her cell, she often thought about the four boxes she had left on the little table, the boxes containing Gab's secret . . . How ironic! There she had done everything she could to open them, and she had been stopped with her hand on the lid. The moment she cleared her name, she would explore the mystery of the cookie tins. That would be her reward.

According to Maître Plessier, the outlook for her trial was positive: the elements of the investigation were in their favor; all the witnesses, with the exception of the shepherd, would be for the defense, and would sit behind the defendant's bench; and as the interrogations proceeded Gabrielle had shown herself to be more and more persuasive, from the police chief to the investigating magistrate.

Because Gabrielle knew perfectly how to tell a convincing lie: all it took was to tell the truth. This she had learned from her father, Paul Chapelier, for as a child she had accompanied him on his concert tours. When this talented conductor was not conducting the musicians himself, he attended other concerts, and because of his fame, he was duty bound to go backstage after the performance to compliment the artists. Mindful not to upset the colleagues with whom he had played or might play, he decided only ever to speak only of what he had appreciated; he tossed out any negative critique, and shared only his positive remarks; and if there was only one single pathetic detail worthy of praise, he would run with it, amplify it, enhance it. Thus, he never lied, except by omission. In his conversations, the performers felt that he was being sincere, and they were free to understand more; the pretentious ones picked up on his enthusiasm, while those who were merely lucid valued his courtesy. To his daughter Paul Chapelier said, more than once: "I don't have enough memory to be a good liar." By saying nothing but the truth and avoiding giving vent to anything at all hurtful, he managed not to contradict himself, and to establish friendships in a milieu that was nevertheless known to be extremely cutthroat.

Gabrielle adopted this method for the two and a half years of her incarceration. When she spoke of Gab, she only ever recalled the radiant period, the period of intense, shared love.

His name was Gabriel, and hers was Gabrielle; together they became Gab and Gaby. The quirks of life and of birth certificates had given them a rare gift: once they were married, they were able to use the same name, give or take one syllable, Gabriel(le) de Sarlat. According to her, this shared identity expressed all their strength as a couple, the indestructibility of their union. To those civil servants who were paid to listen to her, Gabrielle described how she fell in love at first sight with this young man, whom she found shy although he was merely being well brought up; their long flirtation, their escapades, his embarrassed proposal to the artist father whom the boy admired, the ceremony at the Church of the Madeleine where an entire symphony orchestra played for them. Without being asked, she evoked the inviolate attraction of his neat, elegant body, never troubled by fat or middle-age spread, as if a slim shape were an aristocratic quality that came with the handle. She listed their moments of happiness as if saying an endless rosary—the children, the children's marriages, the births of the grandchildren, and despite the passage of time, a man who remained physically intact, with his feelings intact, his gaze upon her unchanged, always bit tentative, respectful, and full of desire. From time to time, she realized that she was making her listeners feel ill at ease, that they were troubled by envy; one day, the examining magistrate went so far as to sigh, "What you are telling me, Madame, is too good to be true."

She looked at him with compassion and murmured, "You must admit, rather, that it is too good for you, Monsieur."

Embarrassed, he did not insist. All the more so as the couple's close family—children, sons-in-law, daughter-in-law, friends, neighbors, all confirmed the idyllic nature of their love. To close the file, the culprit was twice made to sit a lie detector test, which she passed successfully.

Her detention brought with it a solitude that Gabrielle

could only escape from in her memories. As a result, Gab had begun to occupy a more important, extravagant place in her new life as a prisoner: either she was talking about him, or she was thinking about him. It mattered little whether she was isolated or in company: he was there, no one else—kindly, comforting, and faithful.

The problem was that by virtue of hearing only things that were true, she ended up believing them. By hiding the last three years of her life with Gab, and revealing only twenty-seven years of bliss, Gabrielle understood less and less what had happened, what had changed her. She could hardly remember the "trigger," the phrase that had alerted her . . . It was better not to even think about it, anyway, what good would it do! Gaby, because of that "trigger," had proven capable of killing her husband; that woman, the murderess, must not exist until the acquittal; therefore, Gabrielle drowned her in a well of oblivion, severed herself from all the motives and reasons that had led her to bump him off; consequently, she condemned that entire part of her brain.

By virtue of thinking about him so much, she once again became the Gabrielle who was loving and loved, incapable of laying a hand on her husband. Like an actress who is obliged to spend time with her character, who ends up identifying herself with her and shows up unbelievably true to life on the set, Gabrielle showed up at her trial as the inconsolable heroine, the victim of a heinous accusation.

From the first day of the hearing, there was a consensus in her favor. On the second day, reporters were already talking about an unfounded accusation. On the third day, complete strangers in the last row of the overcrowded courtroom were weeping profusely, on the side of the unjustly treated innocent woman. On the fourth day, her children appeared over and over on the television news to express their emotion and indignation.

Gabrielle went through the interrogation and heard the witnesses, paying close attention; she was careful that nothing she said or that others said contradicted the version that she had constructed; she was like a scrupulous composer sitting in on the rehearsals of his work, with the score on his lap.

As anticipated, the shepherd turned out to be fairly catastrophic during his testimony. Not only was his French quite broken—and in this country, an error of syntax or vocabulary does not betray merely a lack of education, it constitutes an aggression against society as a whole, and is tantamount to blasphemy against the national cult of language—but he complained that he had to advance the money for his ticket to "go up to Compiègne," and he grumbled for a good quarter of an hour about the subject. When interrogated by Maître Plissier, he committed the blunder of confessing that he recognized Gabrielle de Sarlat "from her photo in the newspapers," then provided nothing but hateful explanations for his wishy-washy efforts to provide assistance to the body, saying, "For sure if you fall like that, there could'a been nothing left but shreds, no need to go and check, you think I'm stupid, or what?"

With the exception of the shepherd, everything corroborated Gabrielle's innocence. On the last day but one, she relaxed a bit. As a result, when the family doctor came to the witness stand, she did not expect to be so devastatingly affected by what he said.

Dr. Pascal Racan, a loyal friend of the Sarlat couple, told several harmless anecdotes about Gab and Gaby, and among them, there was this:

"I've rarely seen such a loving couple. When one of them decided to do something, it wasn't selfish, it was for the other one. For example, Gaby wanted to go on pleasing her husband, so she took up some sports, and she asked my advice in matters of diet. As for Gab, although he was thin and dry, he still had high blood pressure and he was worried, not about the disease, which could be kept in check with good medication, but about the effects of the treatment. As you know, beta-blockers decrease libido, and diminish sexual appetite. He often came to talk to me about it because he was afraid his wife might think he desired her less. Which was not true, he just didn't feel like it as much. I've never seen a man so worried. I've never known someone so concerned about his companion. In such cases, most men just think about themselves and their health, and when they notice that their appetite is waning, it suits them, it decreases the number of adulterous relations they have; they're delighted to become more virtuous for medical reasons without it costing them any effort. But Gab thought only about Gaby's reaction."

When she heard this hitherto unknown detail, Gabrielle was incapable of restraining a flood of tears. She swore she would be all right in a moment but was so upset that she wasn't, and Maître Plissier had to ask for the hearing to be adjourned, to which the court agreed.

The members of the audience thought they understood why Gabrielle had been so moved. She did not confess anything to Maître Plissier but as soon as she was able to speak again, she voiced a request: "Please, I feel like I'm sinking, I can't keep it up . . . Would you ask my eldest daughter to do me a favor?"

"Yes."

"Have her bring this evening to the prison the four cookie tins that are on a coffee table in her father's room. She will know what I'm talking about."

"I'm not sure that she will have the right to give them to you in the visiting room."

"Oh, I beg you, I shall collapse."

"There, there, only twenty-four hours to go. Tomorrow will be the last day, the speech for the defense. By evening we'll be all set."

"I don't know what they will decide tomorrow, and neither

do you, despite your confidence and your talent. Please, Maître, I can't stand it anymore, I'll do something foolish."

"I don't see how these cookie tins . . ."

"Please. I'm beside myself, I don't know what I might do."

He understood that she was sincere, threatening him, that she might make an attempt on her life. When he saw how over-wrought she was, fearful that she might not make it to the end of the trial, the outcome of which already seemed glorious to him—a red letter day in his career—he dreaded a gaffe and swore that he himself would bring her the boxes she was asking for. Never mind, he would take the risk.

To his utter surprise, because he was not accustomed to such effusiveness from her, Gabrielle took him by the shoulders and kissed him.

The hearing resumed but Gabrielle did not listen; all she could think of was the doctor's testimony, the secret boxes, the "trigger," and everything she had kept silent for two and a half years.

When she was in the van taking her back to the prison, she stretched out her legs and thought.

She had listened to so many people talking about her, and about him, without knowing the facts, that her thoughts were all in a muddle.

Why had she killed him?

Because of the "trigger". . . Was it a mistake?

At the prison, she asked for exceptional permission to go to the shower. Because of her exemplary behavior and the indul-gent treatment the media were giving to her trial, permission was granted.

She slipped under the scorching water. To wash! To cleanse herself of the nonsense she may have said or heard these last days. To think back about what had happened, about the "trigger."

The "trigger" had come from Paulette . . . When that tall, gangly woman with her mannish features first came and settled with her husband in Senlis, she often came to Gabrielle's store to furnish and decorate her new house. Although initially Gabrielle found her vulgar in her appearance—Paulette was as colorful as a parrot in Brazil—and in the way she spoke, she enjoyed her as a customer because she appreciated her insolence, her utter disregard for what people might think, her sharp repartee, incongruous but spot on. Several times, she took her defense against her employees or the customers she frightened off. There was one thing she had to grant her new neighbor: she was very talented at sniffing out any tricky business. Wary and perspicacious at the same time, Paulette brought a number of things to Gabrielle's attention: traffic in fake opalines, then a gang who were dismantling old fireplaces; above all, with a single glance she could detect all the vices and secrets of the other villagers, obscure examples of depravity that Gabrielle herself was unaware of or had taken years to discover. Dazzled by Paulette's clairvoyance, Gabrielle enjoyed spending time with her, sitting on her armchairs that were for sale.

One day, as they were chatting, Gabrielle noticed Paulette's dark gaze—erratic, sidelong—following the movements of an intruder. The object of her scrutiny was none other than Gab, whom Paulette had not met. Amused by the idea of what Paulette would have to say, Gaby did not explain that her beloved husband had just come tearing into the store.

Although their conversation continued seamlessly, Gabrielle was perfectly aware that Paulette was not missing a single thing as she followed Gab's movements, demeanor and expressions.

"What do you think?" asked Gabrielle suddenly, with a wink over in Gab's direction.

"That guy? Oh my God, the perfect two-faced bastard. Too polite to be honest. The hypocrite to end all hypocrites. First prize with a cherry on top."

Gabrielle was so taken aback that her jaw dropped and her mouth stayed open until Gab rushed over to her, kissed her, and greeted Paulette.

As soon as she had realized her blunder, Paulette changed her attitude, and the next day she excused herself for her remark to Gabrielle, but it was too late: the worm was already in the apple.

From that moment on, day by day, Gaby's perception of Gab began to change. If Paulette had made such an assertion, she must have her reasons: she was never wrong! Gaby observed Gab, trying to forget everything she knew about him, or thought she knew, as if he had become a stranger. Worse yet, she tried to justify Paulette's judgment.

To her extreme surprise, it wasn't difficult.

Gab de Sarlat was polite and courteous. He dressed in a casual gentleman farmer style, was always available to help, was a regular churchgoer, had little inclination to overindulge in conversation or ideas, could fascinate and exasperate in equal measure. He was traditional in his feelings, his discourse, and his behavior—and even his physique—and he attracted some people for the same reasons he repelled others, who were not numerous: he looked perfect, ideal.

Caught out by the instinct of the ferocious Paulette, he suddenly posed the same problem to Gabrielle as had two or three pieces of furniture in her life as an antique dealer: original, or imitation? Either you saw him as an honest man who cared about others, or you sniffed out the impostor.

In the space of a few weeks, Gabrielle convinced herself that she was being swindled. If she listed Gab's qualities one by one, she could turn the card over and discover the hidden defect. He was calm? The shell of a hypocrite. He was gallant? A way of channeling an overactive libido and attracting future prey. He dealt thoughtfully with Gabrielle's mood swings? Abysmal indifference. He had married for love—the daring union of a nobleman with a commoner? A contract over money. His Catholic faith? Just another tweed suit, a cloak of respectability. His moral values? Words to hide his impulses. Suddenly, she suspected that the way he helped out in the shop—transporting furniture, either when she bought it or when it was delivered— was just an alibi destined to create free time so that he could move around more discreetly. And what if he used the opportunity to visit his mistresses?

Why, after twenty-seven years of love and trust, did Gabrielle allow herself to be poisoned by doubt? Paulette's venom did not explain everything; no doubt Gabrielle found it difficult, with advancing age, to confront the changes in her body, as she struggled with her weight, her deepening wrinkles, with ever more insistent fatigue, and blood vessels bursting in her once lovely legs . . . If she found it so easy to have her doubts about Gab, it was also because she had doubts about herself, and her powers of attraction. She lost her temper with him because he was aging better than she was, because he was still attractive, because the young girls smiled at him more spontaneously than young men did at her. In society—at the market, the beach, in the street—people still noticed him, whereas Gabrielle had become transparent.

Four months after Paulette's "trigger," Gabrielle could no longer stand him. She could not stand herself either: every morning, her mirror showed her a stranger whom she hated, a big woman with a thick neck, with red blotches on her skin, and cracks in her lips, and flabby arms; she was afflicted with a terrible fold of flesh beneath her belly button which even if she starved herself she could not get rid of, and her diets did not make her any more cheerful. She could not digest the idea that Gab might like this—who could possibly like this? No one!

As a result, all the sweet things—smiles, attention, kindnesses, tender gestures—that Gab offered her the rest of the day were simply hurtful. What a hypocrite! Paulette had hit the nail on the head: a two-faced bastard from the House of Two-Faced Bastards, guaranteed genuine article. In the end, he disgusted her. How could anyone act so unctuously?

The only time he wasn't pretending was when he would exclaim—although his tone remained affectionate—"old girl." Go figure, it just came out! Gabrielle hated it when it happened; every time, she felt a shudder down her back as if she had been whipped.

She began to think about divorce. However, whenever she pictured herself in front of a lawyer or her children, trying to justify the separation, she realized she did not have any sound arguments. They would protest: Gab is wonderful, how can you come out with such nonsense? Her eldest daughter might even send her to see a psychiatrist—she already sent her children to the psychiatrist. She would have to go about it differently.

She decided to find some proof against Gab. "Men—" the peremptory Paulette had claimed, "you have to really push them to the brink to see what they're made of." Gabrielle started changing her mind about everything, saying she wanted to go to such and such a restaurant then refusing, re-setting the date or destination of their holidays fifteen times or more; she added whim to caprice to find him out and make him wild with rage. In vain: every time, he conceded to her demands. At the most, all she might get was a sigh, a gleam of weariness in the back of his eyes in the evening when she behaved abominably. "What has he got in his pants?" Paulette would have said. That was what she herself wondered. For some time now, in bed, if they exchanged tender gestures, not much happened any more. It was true she didn't want it as much as she used to, and she figured that they had copulated plentifully in their life, and that to start at it again after decades was like spending vacation in the same place: boring. And while she had gotten used to it, she gave it some thought and wondered if this peace did not have another meaning for him. Mightn't he be taking advantage of his trips in the van to cheat on her? As a result, she insisted on going along. He said he was delighted and chatted away to his heart's content for the hundreds of miles they covered together during those weeks. At least twice he suggested stopping to make love, once in the back of the car, another time in the middle of a field. And although she accepted, she was devastated. This was the proof! The proof that when he went on his trips, he was used to having his sexual needs met.

She stopped going along on his expeditions, and became morose, communicating less and less, except with Paulette. Her friend could talk forever about men who cheated.

"In this day and age, those cretins get caught by their wives, because they can look at the calls they make or receive on their cell phones. You'd think that private detectives would march in protest against the way cell phones have harmed their business, in the adultery department."

"And if a man doesn't have a cell phone?" asked Gabrielle, thinking about Gab, who refused to let her give him one.

"If a man doesn't have a cell phone, watch out! Red alert! It means he's the king of kings, the emperor of bastards, the prince of abusers. Their sort works the old-fashioned way, he doesn't want to be found out, he uses telephone booths that leave no trace. He knows that adultery was not created at the same time as the cell phone, and he goes on using the well worn tricks he has refined over the years. That kind of guy is the James Bond of illicit sex: you can trail him but you can't catch him. Good luck!"

From then on, Gabrielle became obsessed with the hiding place on the third floor. Gab's secrets had to be there, the proof of his perverse behavior, too. She went there several times with tools, wanting to break down the wall; every time, shame kept her from doing it. Several times she tried to hoodwink Gab by putting on a charm act to convince him to open it for her; every time, he came up with a new excuse to get out of it: "There's nothing in there," "You'll only make fun of me," "You'll have plenty of time to find out what's in there," "Aren't I entitled to my own little secrets?," "It has to do with you but I don't want you to know." All these contradictory refusals annoyed Gabrielle to the extreme, until finally he said, "You'll find out after I'm dead, and that will be soon enough."

His words made her indignant. What did he mean, would she have to wait ten, twenty, thirty years, to have the proof that he had mocked her all her life, and that she had shared her existence with a shifty social climber? Was he trying to provoke her or what?

"You're awfully quiet these days, my dear Gabrielle," exclaimed Paulette when they were drinking tea together.

"I keep my problems to myself. That's the way I was raised. My father stuffed my head with the idea that you should never expose anything but positive thoughts; the other ones you keep silent."

"What bullshit! You have to get it out in the open, sweetheart, otherwise you'll give yourself cancer. Women who keep quiet get cancer. I'll never have cancer because I shout and complain all day long. Never mind if other people don't like it: let them suffer—not me, girl!"

And that is how her plan took shape: she had to free herself of doubt, so she would have to get rid of Gab, a plan she carried out in the Alps.

Gabrielle was taken back into her cell with her wet hair, and she collapsed on the bed to go on thinking. That was what had been going on in her brain for the last three years of their life together as a couple, that was what she was hiding from everyone, that was how her life had been drained of savor and meaning to be reduced to a continuous nightmare. At the least by killing Gab she had acted, had put an end to that unbearable anxiety. She didn't regret it. This afternoon, however, the doctor's testimony had shaken her: she had learned why Gab was no longer as sensual, and how he must be suffering. The doctor's comment had chipped away at her block of convictions.

Why was she discovering this only now? Before, she used to think he avoided her to devote his energy to his mistresses. Couldn't that irresponsible Dr. Racan have spoken to her about it earlier?

"Gabrielle de Sarlat to the visitors' room. Your lawyer is waiting for you."

It couldn't have come at a better time.

Maître Plissier placed the four tin boxes on the table.

"There you are! Now, explain."

Gabrielle didn't answer. She sat down and opened the tins, voraciously. Her fingers scurried through the papers that lay inside each box, pulling some sheets out to decipher them, then others, and still others . . .

After a few minutes, Gabrielle fell to the floor, prostrate, suffocating. Maître Plissier alerted the warders, who helped him to make the prisoner comfortable and got her to breathe. They took her on a stretcher to the infirmary, where they gave her a tranquilizer.

An hour later, when she had regained consciousness, she asked where her lawyer had gone. They informed her that he had gone away again with the boxes to prepare for the hearing.

Gabrielle begged them to give her another tranquilizer, and lapsed into unconsciousness. Anything, rather than think about what those metal boxes contained.

The next morning prosecution and defense stated their case. Gabrielle resembled a vague memory of herself—pale, gaunt, her eyes full of tears, her complexion blotchy, her lips drained of blood. If she had been striving consciously to gain the sympathy of the jurors, she could not have done a better job.

The prosecutor gave a summing up that was more determined than it was harsh, and it impressed no one. Then Maître
Plissier, his sleeves quivering, got up like a soloist called on
stage to give his bravura performance.

"What happened? A man died in the mountains. Let us
leave the act aside for a moment and consider the two opposing
versions that have brought us before the court: an accident, says
his wife; an assassination, claims a shepherd, a stranger. Let us
stand farther back still, let us stand very far back, at least as far
back as the shepherd, if it is possible to see anything clearly at
such a distance, and now let us examine the motives for murder.
There are none! As a rule, I find it difficult to exercise my pro-
fession as a lawyer because everything seems to point to the
guilt of the person I am defending. In the case of Gabrielle
Sarlat, there is nothing to point to her guilt, nothing! No
motives, no grounds. There was no money at stake. No tension
in their relation. No betrayals. Nothing to suggest she is guilty,
except for one thing. A man. That is, a man who lives with animals, a boy who can neither read nor write, who rebelled
against his schooling, who was incapable of belonging to society
in any way other than to isolate himself from it. In short, this
shepherd, an employee whom I could easily accuse because he
was let go by several employers, a worker who satisfied no one,
a man who has neither wife nor children; in short, this shepherd
saw her. How far away was he standing? Not two hundred
yards, nor three hundred, a distance which would already be a
handicap to anyone's vision—but a mile, according to the find-
ings of the reconstruction! Let us be serious, ladies and gentlemen of the jury, what can you see from a mile away?
Personally, nothing. The shepherd, a crime. It's extraordinary,
no? Moreover, after he has witnessed the murder, he does not
rush to help the victim, he does not call for a rescue party or the
police. Why? According to his allegations, because he cannot
leave his herd. This is an individual who watches as a fellow

human being is being murdered, but who goes on thinking that the life of his animals—who will end up on a skewer—is more important . . . I cannot understand this man, ladies and gentlemen of the jury. It would not matter so seriously if he were not accusing an admirable woman, a spouse of integrity, an exemplary mother, incriminating her of the very last thing she would have wanted, the death of her Gabriel, Gabriel nicknamed Gab, the love of her life."

He turned abruptly to face the jurors.

"Well, you may object, ladies and gentlemen of the jury, that nothing is ever as it seems! Even if everybody attests to their love, so strong and so visible, what was going on in their minds? This woman, Gabrielle de Sarlat, may have been corroded with suspicion, jealousy, doubt. Who can prove that she did not suffer from a paranoid neurosis regarding her spouse? In addition to all the witnesses you heard here and who did not offer the slightest justification for such a hypothesis, I would like to add, ladies and gentlemen of the jury, my own testimony. Do you know what this woman did, last night? Do you know the only favor she asked of me in two and a half years of custody? She asked me to bring her four cookie tins in which for over thirty years she had been storing their letters, as well as the mementos of their love. Everything can be found in there, theater and concert tickets, the menus from their engagement party and their wedding, and all the birthdays, little notes they wrote to each other and left on the kitchen table in the morning—from the ordinary to the sublime, everything! Thirty years. Up until the last day. Up until they left on their tragic vacation. The warders will confirm that she then spent hours, in tears, thinking about the man she had lost. I ask you, and this will be my last question, does an assassin do such a thing?"

Gabrielle collapsed on her chair while her children, and the more sensitive souls in the gallery, could hardly contain their tears.

The court and the jury withdrew to deliberate.

In the corridor where she was waiting on the bench next to Maître Plissier, Gabrielle thought about the letters she had read the night before. There was one that showed her that from the time of their youth, he had always called her "old girl"—how could she have forgotten, and taken the expression for a cruel mockery? Another where he described her, twenty-five years earlier, as "my violent, wild, secret, unpredictable woman." That is what he thought of the woman who would kill him, "violent and unpredictable": how right he was, poor man. So, he really had loved her the way she was, with her quick temper, her rages and angers and spells of the blues, her ruminations, and he was so calm that these storms merely amused him.

And so her husband's secret had been her own self.

In her imagination she had destroyed their love. Alas, it was not in her imagination that she had pushed him into the void.

Why had she given so much importance to what Paulette said? How could she have stooped to the level of that sordid woman, who saw the world in such an abject, petty way? No, it was too easy to accuse Paulette. She was the guilty one. She alone. No one else. Her most powerful argument for losing her trust in Gab had been: "It is impossible for a man to love the same woman for more than thirty years." Now, she understood that the true argument, between the lines of the first one, had been, rather: "It is impossible for me to love the same man for more than thirty years." Guilty, Gabrielle de Sarlat! The only culprit!

A bell. Commotion. Excitement. The trial was starting again. It was like going back to the races after an intermission.

"To the question: 'Does the jury find that the accused deliberately took the life of her husband?' the jurors have replied, unanimously, 'no.'"

A murmur of approval went through the courtroom.

"All charges against Gabrielle de Sarlat have been dropped. Madame, you are free to go," concluded the judge.

Gabrielle lived through what followed in a haze. They kissed her, congratulated her, her children wept for joy, Maître Plissier strutted and preened. To thank him, she declared that when she heard his defense, she had felt deep inside what he was saying: it was impossible, unthinkable, for a woman as blessed and fulfilled in her marriage as she was to commit such an act. Deep inside herself, she added that it was another woman, a stranger, an unknown person who had nothing to do with her.

To those who asked her how she planned to spend her time in the days ahead, she did not reply. She knew she had to spend it in mourning for a wonderful man. Had they any idea that a mad woman, two and a half years earlier, had taken her husband from her? Would she be able to live without him? To survive such violence?

One month after her acquittal, Gabrielle de Sarlat left her home in Senlis, went back to the Alps, and rented a room at the Hôtel des Adrets, not far from the Hôtel Bellevue where she had stayed with her husband the last time.

In the evening, on the tiny desk in white pine that was next to her bed, she wrote a letter.

My dear children,
Even though the trial ended with the declaration of my inno-
cence, and it acknowledged that it would be impossible for me to
kill a man as marvelous as your father Gabriel, the only man I
have ever loved, it made his disappearance seem all the more
unbearable. Understand my sorrow. Forgive me for taking leave
of you. I need to be with him.

The next morning, she walked back up to the col de l'Aigle and, from the path where she had pushed her husband two and a half years earlier, she leapt into the void.

GETTING BETTER

Lucky me, to have such a pretty woman looking after me..."
The first time he muttered those words, she thought she had misheard and she was angry with herself. How could she transform a patient's complaint into a compliment? If her subconscious played the trick on her again, she would go to see a psychoanalyst. It was out of the question for her complexes to keep her from working! It was already bad enough that they kept her from living . . .

Disgruntled, in the hours that followed, as soon as she had a moment of respite from her tasks, Stéphanie tried to work out what the patient in room 221 might have actually said. The beginning of the sentence must have been correct, *lucky me, to have . . .* but she wasn't sure about the end. *Pretty woman?* No one had ever called Stéphanie a pretty woman. And with good reason, she thought.

By the time she left the Hôpital de la Salpêtrière that day, the young nurse had not uncovered the answer. She wandered thoughtfully beneath a sky heavy with rain, almost black, between tall steep towers; at their foot, the avenues bordered by thin acacia trees seemed flat and empty. She lived in a studio in Chinatown, to the south of Paris, a neighborhood with grayish green walls and red shop signs. She felt huge in these streets full of Asians, next to these small, delicate women, busy ants going about their business. Not only did her size—normal—transform her into a giant, but her curves seemed excessive next to these lithe figures.

In the evening, she could not concentrate on the endless nauseating stream of television programs, so she threw down the remote and turned to her highly suspicious, insistent thoughts.

"'Lucky me, to have such a pretty woman looking after me!' My poor Stéphanie, you are looking for one sentence under another because it allows you to repeat the one you liked; but he didn't say the one you liked. So in reality, you're not making anything clearer, you're just rehashing your thoughts to flatter yourself and indulge."

At that point she put in a big load of washing—something that always calmed her—and set about ironing her "backlog of laundry." On the radio they were playing songs from her childhood, one after the other, so she turned up the volume and enjoyed a happy moment, steam iron in hand, wailing the refrains she remembered.

At midnight, after she'd done several piles of clothes, she had sung so much that her head was spinning and she saw stars dancing behind her eyelids, so she went to bed feeling serene, and thought she had forgotten everything.

However, the next morning she trembled as she crossed the threshold of room 221.

He was so handsome it made you start.

Karl Bauer had already been in intensive care for over a week, and was emerging from shock. Part of his spinal column had been crushed in a car accident, so the doctors doubted he would recover, but they wouldn't certify anything; for the time being, they were stimulating his nerves, trying to determine the extent of the damage.

Although he was lying under a sheet and a bandage covered his eyes, everything she could see of his face or body affected Stéphanie deeply. His hands, to begin with: the long hands of a man, elegant, with oval, almost mother of pearl nails, hands made to hold precious objects or caress a lock of hair . . . And the color of him, his dark skin, the brown shadow of fine hair on his taut muscles, the luminous black of his curls. And his full, well-shaped mouth, that seemed to draw your gaze . . . And that nose above all, like a blade of flesh, precise and strong, alluring, so manly that Stéphanie could not look at it without feeling something stirring below her belly.

He was tall. Even lying down. They had had to bring a special bed up from the basement to fit his body. Despite his immobility, and the tubes hanging everywhere, his size impressed Stéphanie, because it seemed to confirm his splendid manliness.

"I fancy him so much I can't think straight. If he were ugly, I would never have deformed his words yesterday."

Today she kept her ears open, the better to understand him. While she was dosing the IV, and counting his pills, he woke up and sensed her presence.

"Are you there?"

"Hello, I'm Stéphanie."

The wings of his nose were quivering. Taking advantage of her invisibility, Stéphanie observed his nostrils, so curiously endowed with their own life.

"Did you come already yesterday morning?"

"Yes."

"I'm glad you're here, Stéphanie."

His lips parted in a smile.

Stéphanie stood there silently. She was touched that such a severely injured man, who must be suffering a martyrdom, could be so tactful as to voice his thanks. He was not your usual patient.

"Maybe that's what he said yesterday," she thought, "something nice, surprising. Yes, that must have been it."

Calmer, she continued the conversation, talking eagerly about little things, the treatments they had in store, the organization of his day, the fact that the next day he would be allowed to have visits. After babbling for ten minutes, Stéphanie deemed that she had managed to recover her normal behavior.

And so she was absolutely paralyzed when he exclaimed, "How lucky I am, to have a pretty woman looking after me."

This time, she was sure of what she had heard. No she wasn't crazy. The identical words, yesterday, and today. And he was talking to her.

Stéphanie leaned over Karl to check the expression on his face: a voluptuous contentment spread over his features, confirming what he had said; his lips were swelling like breasts; he even gave her the impression he was looking at her with pleasure, despite his blindfolded eyes.

What could she do? She was incapable of continuing their conversation. Respond to his compliment? What might he add? How far would it lead them?

These questions tumbling over one another upset her, and she fled from the room.

Out in the corridor, she burst into tears.

When she found Stéphanie on the floor, her colleague Marie-Thérèse, a black woman from Martinique, helped her to her feet, handed her a handkerchief, then led her into a discreet little room where bandages were stored.

"Tell me, honey, what's going on?"

This unexpected tenderness merely doubled Stéphanie's sorrow; she sobbed against her colleague's soft, round shoulder. She would never have stopped if the smell of vanilla wafting from Marie-Thérèse's skin hadn't calmed her, reminding her of childhood happiness, birthday parties at her grandparents', or yogurt evenings at the house of her neighbor Emma.

"So tell me, what is making you so sad?"

"I don't know."

"Is it work or private life?"

"Both," moaned Stéphanie, sniffling.

She blew her nose noisily to put an end to her ludicrous behavior.

"Thank you, Marie-Thérèse, I feel much better now."

Although her eyes remained dry for the rest of the day, she did not feel better, particularly as she could not understand what this crisis was about.

At the age of twenty-five, Stéphanie had studied to become a nurse, but she did not know herself well. Why not? Because she was wary of her own self, a distance she had inherited from a mother who did not look kindly on her daughter. How could she give her own self any importance when the person who had brought her into this world, and who was supposed to love her, denigrated her? Léa, in fact, found her daughter neither pretty nor intelligent, and she never missed an opportunity to tell her so. And each time, she would add, "What do you expect, it's not because I'm a mother that I'm not allowed to be lucid!" The mother's opinion, slightly altered, controlled the daughter's opinion. And while Stéphanie had managed to overcome her mother's mockery as far as intelligence was concerned—Léa had no diploma, and continued to sell clothes, whereas Stéphanie had passed her baccalaureate and managed to complete her paramedical training—in the visual realm she had adopted her mother's aesthetic canon without question. Since a beautiful woman had to be slender, with narrow hips and breasts like apples, just like Léa herself, well, then Stéphanie was not a beautiful woman; she figured, rather—as her mother often repeated—in the fat lump category. She weighed twenty-five pounds more than her mother, although she was only three inches taller.

As a result, Stéphanie had always rejected Léa's offers to "make her over," fearful that she would only add insult to injury. Convinced that lace, silk, braids, chignons, curls, jewels, bracelets, earrings, or necklaces would look as shocking on her as on a transvestite, she knew she was a woman physiologically, but she did not hold herself to be any more feminine than a man. Her white hospital scrubs suited her, and when she hung them up in the locker at the hospital, it was only to replace them with their black or navy blue equivalent, while she swapped her orthopedic clogs for a pair of thick white running shoes.

What had happened in room 221? Joy or despair? The joy of being considered pretty? The despair that her only admirer was a blind man?

In reality, Stéphanie's emotion—she grasped this as she slid under her comforter—came above all from the shock: his words had placed her back on the market for seduction—that vast, sunny square where women are attractive to men—and here she had thought she was excluded, living off on her own the way she did, determined never to elicit a man's gaze or a declaration of love. Stéphanie was a well-behaved young lady, if you can call "well-behaved" someone who has never known misbehaving. Her complexes left her austere, and she dared not try anything, but fled from parties, bars, and nightclubs. To be sure, she might dream about a love affair, for the duration of a film or a novel, but she remained well aware that it was merely a fantasy. Things like that didn't happen in real life.

"At least, not in my life."

Like an old man who is used to his retirement, she had pictured herself as peaceful, out of reach, endowed with a body that was dead, or almost, and now here was someone upsetting her, talking about her charm. It was unexpected, abrupt, jarring.

The next morning as she was walking to work she decided that if Karl started up again, she would rebuff him.

The hospital routinely filled her life. The moment she went through the door at the Salpêtrière, guarded like military barracks, she entered another world, a city within a city, her city. And behind the enclosure that protected this medical citadel with its high walls there was everything: a newspaper kiosk, a café, a chapel, a pharmacy, a cafeteria, social services, administrative offices, and meeting rooms, in addition to the numerous buildings devoted to various pathologies; in the gardens there were benches for weary strollers, and a few flowerbeds, and birds hopping in the grass; the seasons passed here as elsewhere, with winter leaving its snow, and summer its heat waves; holidays marked the passage of time— Christmas trees, the solstice; people came here to be born, to get better, to die; sometimes they even saw famous people. A microcosm in the megalopolis. Not only did Stéphanie feel she existed, here, but she also proved herself useful. One hour followed closely upon the next, busy with care, visits, trips to the infirmary, temperature taking: why should she need another life, a life elsewhere?

The feeling that she was being useful gave her a pride that made up for anything that might be missing. "I don't have time to think about myself, I have too much to do," she would say to herself whenever she caught a glimpse of her solitude.

"Good morning, Stéphanie," said Karl with a smile, although she had only just come in, and hadn't said a thing.

"Good morning. You are finally going to get some visits today."

"So I fear."

"Why? Aren't you glad?"

"Sparks will fly!"

"What do you mean?"

"From your point of view, it will probably be rather amusing. Somewhat less so for them than for me."

"Who do you mean, them?"

"Can't you guess?"

"No."

"Well then, be patient, you're in for a show."

Stéphanie decided to drop the subject and set to work.

He was smiling.

The busier she got around the bed, the bigger his smile.

After she had sworn she would not ask, she eventually gave in and exclaimed, "Why are you smiling like that?"

"A pretty woman is looking after me . . ."

"What do you know? You can't see me!"

"I can hear you and I can sense you."

"Excuse me?"

"From your voice, your movements, the air you displace with your gestures, and above all your smell, I can tell that you are a pretty woman. I'm sure of it."

"You're teasing me! What if I have a wart on my nose or a birthmark?"

"That would surprise me."

"Will you bet on it?"

"All right: do you have a wart on your nose?"

"No."

"A birthmark?"

"Not that either."

"Well!" he concluded, glad that he was right.

Stéphanie gave a laugh and left the room.

Unlike the day before, she continued her day in a good mood, having recovered her cheerful nature.

That afternoon as she went from one room to the next, she understood what Karl had meant earlier that day—it was funny, no, the way he wrote his name with a K rather than a C? In the waiting room, seven young women, each one more magnificent than the next, were glaring at each other with hatred; they looked like a lineup of models competing for a shoot. Not one of them had an official tie with Karl except for the tall striking redhead, who was boasting to the head nurse that she was the "ex-wife," and thus obtained priority. The six others—the mistresses—shrugged their shoulders as they saw her go away and continued glaring at each other in an exceedingly unfriendly way. Had they just found out about each other? Were they successive mistresses or simultaneous mistresses?

Stéphanie did what she could to go by there as often as possible, but she didn't manage to find out anything more. The moment they left their seat to go to see Karl, they all went through the same rigmarole: in one second, as soon as they headed down the corridor, they left behind their glower to put on a face that was ravaged with anguish, eyes damp with tears, handkerchief in hand. What actresses! Besides, which was the actual performance? Their masterful self-control in each other's presence, or the trembling arrival at their lover's bedside? Were they ever sincere?

The last one went into the room at four o'clock and came out a minute later screaming, "He's dead! My God, he just died!"

Stéphanie rushed out of the office, ran up to the bed, grabbed Karl's pulse, looked at the monitors and exclaimed, "Be quiet! He's asleep, that's all. He's exhausted by all these visits. In his condition . . ."

The mistress sat down squeezing her knees, as if that would make her feel better. She bit the nail on her thumb which was long and red, then she fussed, "Those bitches, they did it on purpose! They wore him out so there'd be nothing left for me!"

"Look, Mademoiselle, you don't seem to realize, this is a man who has just survived a very serious accident. All you can think about is yourself and your rivals, it's indecent!"

"Who do you think you are? Are you being paid to take care of him or to lecture us about morality?"

"To take care of him. Therefore, I have to ask you to leave."

"Fuck off! I waited four hours."

"Right. I'm calling security."

Grumbling, the supermodel yielded to the threat, and stalked off, wobbling on her high platform heels.

Stéphanie gave a mental shout of "Bitch!", then devoted herself to Karl, raising his bed, plumping his pillows, checking his IV, not at all sorry to have him to herself again.

"At last I can get some work done," she sighed. Not for a moment did it cross her mind that she had just reacted like a jealous woman.

The next morning, Karl greeted her with a smile.

"Well, did you have fun, yesterday?"

"What was fun about it?"

"Making those women who hate each other sit down and wait patiently in each other's presence. Frankly, I was sorry to be in here and not in the waiting room. Did the fur fly over there?"

"No, but they did transform the waiting room into an ice box. Did you hear me send the last one away?"

"The last one? No. Who came after Dora?"

"A brunette on platform heels."

"Samantha? Oh, I'm sorry, I would have liked to see her."

"Well, you couldn't."

"What was wrong with me?"

"You fell asleep! She thought you were dead."

"Samantha always exaggerates."

"I took the liberty of telling her that."

While she was attending to him, a thousand questions assailed her brain. Which of the six mistresses was the current one? Was there one he loved? What did he expect from a woman? Was it because he only chose them for their looks, without expecting anything more, that he bounced from one to the other? Did he only go for erotic liaisons, never any lasting relationship? Did he take the initiative with women? Did he rely for a large part on his own physical powers of attraction? What type of lover might he be?

As if he had sensed all the agitation in her brain, Karl exclaimed, "You seem to be somewhat preoccupied today!"

"Me? Oh, no."

"Oh, yes. A problem with your husband?"

"I'm not married."

"Your partner?"

"No partner, either."

"Your boyfriend, then?"

"Yes, that's it, a problem with my boyfriend."

To a man who thought she must be ravishing, she did not have the heart to confess to her hopeless solitude, so she decided to invent a fiancé for herself: at least here, in room 221, she could be a normal woman.

"What's he done?"

"Hmm . . . Nothing . . . Nothing for sure . . . I wonder if . . . I wonder if he isn't having an affair . . ."

"Are you jealous?"

Stéphanie didn't know what to say. Not only was she not used to being asked such a question, but she just realized that she was jealous of Karl.

She said nothing. He laughed.

"So, you are jealous!"

"Who isn't?"

"I am not, for one, however I prefer not to talk about it. Let's get back to you. What's his name?"

Stéphanie would have liked to reply, but all she could think of were names of dogs, Rex, Titus, Médor, Tommy . . . In a panic, she managed to blurt, "Ralf!"

Of course, that was also a dog's name, a Doberman that she ran into from time to time, but she hoped that Karl would not suspect anything. Ralf, that could be a human name, couldn't it?

"Well Ralf is a fool, if you want my opinion."

Phew, he'd swallowed it.

"You don't know him."

"When a man meets a woman as gorgeous as you, who smells so lovely, the first thing he does is move in with her. And you've just told me you don't live together."

"Don't blame him! Perhaps I'm the one who doesn't want to . . ."

"You don't want to?"

"That's not it either."

"So I'll repeat what I said, Ralf is a fool. He doesn't deserve you. To be apart from a woman with such a scent . . ."

Stéphanie panicked. What scent? In twenty-five years, she had never imagined she gave off any odor . . . Instinctively, she moved her nose toward her arm. What scent? She couldn't smell a thing. What was he talking about? She didn't use perfume or eau de toilette. Could it be her soap? And yet that vanished so quickly . . . Her washing powder? The softener? No, all the hospital personnel got their laundry cleaned by the same company. Her smell? Her own smell? Was it a good or a bad smell? Above all, what did it smell like?

She could only hold back for about thirty seconds, then she asked, breathless, "What do I smell like? Sweat?"

"Now you're being funny! No, I have no idea what your sweat is like—and good job, too, it must be divine, I'd get too excited."

"Are you joking?"

"I assure you, you have an intoxicating scent and if Ralf never told you so, Ralf is most definitely a stupid jerk."

That evening, when she was back in her studio, Stéphanie tried one experiment after another.

After she had drawn the curtains, she undressed and, sitting on her bed, tried to smell herself. She put her nostrils up to every part of her body she could get at. Before taking her shower, she went into contortions, and then again afterwards. In vain.

Nevertheless, although she despised being naked, she didn't get dressed again and tried, rather, another method: she endeavored to intercept her smell in her wake, by turning around quite abruptly; the moment she had taken three steps, she spun on her heels and hurried with her nose in the air on her own trace, with the impression that she was performing a ballet. And while she didn't manage to capture anything at all, she found great pleasure in walking like this, with her thighs and her breasts in the air.

For dinner, intimidated by the pomp of plate and cutlery, she put on a bathrobe; however as she ate, she opened it somewhat, until finally she stepped out of it, hoping once again to snatch her smell.

Finally, she investigated her wardrobe, sniffing the clothes she had worn, comparing them with what she hadn't worn, then going back to the first . . . She did notice something, but it was almost nothing, a subtle essence, evanescent, that escaped the moment she thought she had grasped it.

She decided to sleep naked. That way when she woke up she could find her smell in the sheets. But after an hour of tossing this way and that, and feeling herself, and checking her curves, she concluded that nudity was driving her crazy, so she put on her pajamas and gradually lost consciousness.

The next morning she went silently into the room and walked up to the bed without giving Karl any warning.

After thirty seconds, he smiled. A moment later, he mumbled, a note of concern in his voice, "Stéphanie?"

She would have liked for the game to last a bit longer, but a syringe rolled on her metal tray, revealing her presence.

"Yes."

He sighed with relief.

"You were here?"

"For a minute. I didn't want to wake you."

"I wasn't asleep. Now I understand why I was obsessing about you."

They chatted while Stéphanie examined her patient. She tried a new experiment. As she had noticed that whenever she walked up behind him, spreading her arms, he smiled, she came closer, put her breasts above his face. Victory! Karl's features radiated with pleasure. She concluded that he wasn't lying: she really did give off a scent that enchanted him.

She amused herself by trying again, going closer this time. At one point, her hair caressed his cheek. What would her colleagues think if they saw her bending over him like this? Who cared! She was so happy to see his superb face light up with joy.

At the end, when she told him, placing her décolleté beneath his nostrils, that she was going to look after her other patients, he mumbled as if he were in a swoon, "What bliss to have such a pretty woman looking after me . . ."

"You're exaggerating, I'm no dream girl, far from it!"

"A dream girl is not the one a girl dreams of being, but the one a boy sees."

On Saturday and Sunday she was off. She missed Karl. She went from one state to the next. On the one hand, she went on walking around her apartment naked to try to grow accustomed to something she'd never before been aware of: the good smells of her own body. On the other hand, she cried a great deal because a bold venture into a Chinese shop selling embroidered silk had destroyed her dream and brought her back to reality: nothing suited her, she was fat and ugly.

So to avoid the gaze of others she locked herself away, eating out of cans, talking only with her television set. Why weren't other men as refined as Karl? Why did society continue to favor the sense of sight over others? In a different world, in the olfactory world, she was admirable. In a different world, she had the power to bewitch. In a certain room that she knew, she was "such a pretty woman." She waited for Monday morning as if for a deliverance.

"Do you realize what you are telling yourself, my poor Stéphanie? You're nothing but a prime cut of meat for a paralyzed blind man. What a disaster!"

After joyfulness came despondency.

And so she spent two days hovering between lamentation and ecstasy, pathos and enthusiasm. Consequently, when the hospital called her on Sunday evening to ask her to come in early the next day, she eagerly accepted.

Just after dawn, teams met at the cafeteria to take over from one another around a cappuccino, the last one for some, the first for others, while the daytime caregivers replaced the night-time ones. There was a vague moment, blue and gray, in the buildings, a moment like a suspended silence, and then the transformation took place: in the time it took for a bitter sip while exchanging a few words, suddenly it was daytime, with the noise of carts, doors slamming, shoes squeaking, the to and fro on each floor, vacuum cleaners humming in the stairway, admissions employees opening their desks on the ground floor. Another rhythm throbbed along the corridors, time to wake up the patients, to take their temperature, hand out their pills, the sound of cups and saucers banging.

At half past seven, fresh, alert and jubilant, Stéphanie rushed into Karl's room.

"Good morning," she said.

"What? You, Stéphanie, already?" said the man with the bound eyes, astonished.

"Yes, me already. One of my colleagues is sick—I know, people are always surprised when a nurse or a doctor has problems with their health. So I have to take over for her."

"And I'll take over for myself: I'll play at being a patient. Apparently I do it quite well."

"You do it very well."

"Alas . . ."

"What I meant is that you never complain."

"What would be the point?"

The morning fog still clung to the windowpanes.

Stéphanie wrote down his temperature, changed his drip,

modified a few doses then gave him a shot. She stuck her head into the corridor to call the nurse's aide.

"Madame Gomez, come and help me with the bath!"

Behind her, Karl objected violently: "You're not going to inflict that on me, are you?"

"What?"

"Bathe me?"

Stéphanie walked over to him, not understanding.

"Yes, we are, why?"

He grimaced, annoyed, his face turning from right to left as if he were looking for help.

"I . . . I don't like the idea!"

"Don't worry, I'm used to it."

As Madame Gomez came in, he didn't insist. Assuming that she had reassured him, Stéphanie picked up a washcloth and a bottle of liquid soap.

Madame Gomez pulled back the sheet to uncover Karl, and Stéphanie could not help but be affected. She thought he was beautiful. Completely beautiful. There was nothing to dislike about his body. It all filled her with emotion.

Although he was injured and could not move, there was nothing to indicate that he was an invalid.

She looked away. For the first time, she thought she didn't have the right to look at a man's nudity without his consent; with hindsight, Madame Gomez's movements to undress Karl, sheets raised quickly by an indifferent hand, seemed violent.

Where should she begin?

Although she knew the movements by heart, for having repeated them hundreds of times, Karl's presence intimidated her. It was his thighs, his torso, his stomach, his shoulders that she was about to touch. Ordinarily, she would clean a patient the way she would wipe a sponge over a plastified tablecloth; with him it was different, he intimidated her. Without the pretext of the hospital, she would never have seen him naked. Even if he did attribute an exquisite scent to her, he would never choose her as a mistress, would he?

Without scruples, Madame Gomez had begun to scrub on her side.

Stéphanie did not want anyone to suspect how reticent she felt, so she set to work. However, her rubbing was softer, more enveloping.

"What are you doing, poor idiot?" she thought. "He's paralyzed. Paralyzed! That means he cannot feel your hand. Whether you pinch him or caress him, the effect is identical: that is, there is none."

Emboldened by the thought, she concentrated on details in order to complete the job; however, she was unwise enough to look at his face and she noticed that he was grinding his teeth, his jaws clenched, and shivering all over. Then, as she was massaging his neck, he murmured in an imperceptible voice, "I am sorry."

She heard so much distress in his whisper that she ordered Madame Gomez to reply to the bell from room 209.

"I'll finish off, Madame Gomez, it's okay."

Once they were alone, she leaned over and questioned him gently.

"Sorry? Why are you sorry?"

"I'm sorry," he repeated, turning his head from right to left.

She wondered what was happening to him, and looked up and down his body and suddenly understood the reason for his distress.

His sex was standing bolt upright.

Stéphanie could not help but admire his solid member, sheathed in fine skin; such an erection was a tribute to him, and seemed to her both strong and gentle; then she went back to her chore, shook her thoughts from her mind, and understood that she had to reassure Karl.

"Don't you worry. We're used to it. It's an automatic reflex."

"No!"

"Yes, don't worry, I know what it is."

He responded angrily, "No, you don't know what it is! Not for a second! And don't say just anything: automatic reflex . . . When someone touches me below my chin, I feel nothing. When your colleague Antoinette looks after me, I'm relaxed, I don't need to clench my teeth. Why? Because Antoinette and Madame Gomez don't have the same smell as you do. I tried to warn you . . ."

"Oh go on . . . It's no big deal . . ."

"If it's not a big deal, then what is?" he exclaimed in a broken voice.

"Don't be embarrassed, I'm not," she lied.

"You're not embarrassed? Thank you! Now I understand that I really am nothing more than an invalid!"

Stéphanie saw tears wetting the bandage on his eyes. She felt like holding Karl close to her to console him, but it wasn't allowed. If she were caught like that, a naked man in the arms of a nurse, with him in that state! Not to mention that if she enveloped him in her smell, it would only get worse . . .

"What have I done, dear Lord, what have I done!" she cried.

Karl changed. His body began to shake violently. He was moaning. Stéphanie was going to call for help when she suspected what was happening.

"Are you . . . are you laughing?"

He confirmed that he was by continuing to shake.

When she saw that his sex was decreasing in size, proportionately to his growing hilarity, Stéphanie was relieved and, infected by his laughter, began to giggle uncontrollably.

She covered his body with a sheet and sat down next to him, just long enough to catch her breath.

When eventually he had calmed down, Stéphanie asked, "What was so funny?"

"The way you cried out, as if there were some catastrophe, 'Dear Lord, what have I done?' when in fact you had given me a hard on. Can you imagine how absurd the situation is?"

They laughed uproariously.

"Let's be serious now. No more humiliation. No more bathing with you. Do you understand?"

"I understand."

In actual fact, Stéphanie was not sure she understood; what she had realized was that she had this power, this new power, this stupefying power to arouse desire in a man. What am I saying? To arouse desire in this man, this very man, this splendid man, this man whom women swarm over, the kind of man sublime mistresses fight over! She had such a power—a fat, ill-favored woman!

For the rest of the day she avoided room 221 because it seemed like her colleagues were on to something, because they were looking at her strangely. In spite of herself, she did feel different, she could not help but act more volubly, more exuberantly than usual, with a blush coming to her cheeks on the slightest pretext.

"My word, Stéphanie, are you in love, by any chance?" asked Marie-Thérèse in her cheerful singsong accent, rolling her r's and drawling her vowels.

Overwhelmed by a flush of heat, Stéphanie did not answer, but smiled, and ran off to the pharmacy.

"She's fallen in love," concluded Marie-Thérèse, nodding her head.

And yet Marie-Thérèse was wrong: Stéphanie had not fallen in love, she had just become a woman.

That night, she got undressed. Far from hiding from her mirror, she stood right in front of it.

"You're attractive! You can be attractive!"

She was announcing this to her body like good news, or a reward.

"This body can arouse a man," she said to her reflection.

Her reflection didn't look terribly convinced.

"Yes!" she insisted. "No later than this morning . . ."

She told her image what had happened that morning, relating in detail the power of her smell . . .

After she finished her story, she put on a bathrobe, had dinner, and dived into bed to think about it, and then think about it some more.

On Tuesday at dawn, as soon as she arrived in the changing room, she negotiated with Madame Gomez to get her to accept, in exchange for small favors—never suspecting a thing—to take care of bathing the patient in room 221.

And then, once Karl had been washed, she went into the room.

"Thank you for not coming," he sighed.

"That's the first time anyone's ever said that to me!"

"It's strange, isn't it? There are some people around whom you couldn't care less about being indecent, but others not. No doubt because you want them to like you."

"You want me to like you?" she asked, her throat tight.

While waiting for his reply, she began to feel faint.

"Yes I'd like that. At least, I would have liked that."

"You win! I do like you."

She went up to him, and brushed her lips against his.

"Am I dreaming, or did you just kiss me?" he exclaimed.

"You're dreaming."

All day long, she kept the memory of that contact on her lips. How could it possibly be so good?

While she forced herself not to neglect her other patients, she did spend more time in Karl's room—or was it just that time went by more quickly there. The moment she was over the threshold of room 221, she went through an invisible barrier and found herself in a different world.

At around noon, while Karl and Stéphanie were talking about trivial things, he broke off, and changed the subject.

"How do you dress when you're not at the hospital?"

She crossed off reality with one bold stroke, thinking of her shapeless clothes waiting in the changing room, or her closets at home, and she decided to lie.

"Skirts."

"Ah, so much the better."

"Yes, skirts and blouses. Silk, if possible. Sometimes a skirt with a suit jacket. In summer, light dresses . . ."

"Ravishing. And in winter?"

Stéphanie blushed, thinking of the outrageous thing she was about to say.

"I like to wear leather. Not bikers' leather, sophisticated leather, glamorous, do you know what I mean?"

"I adore that! What a pity I can't see you."

"Here we wear hospital scrubs for work. Not very sexy."

"Even on you?"

"Even on me."

"I doubt that. Anyway, you get your revenge elsewhere."

"That's right . . . I get my revenge . . ."

In the afternoon, on leaving the hospital, she decided to make true what only that morning had been a falsehood, and she headed for the department stores on the Boulevard Haussmann.

To get there she took the métro, which was something she rarely did, because Stéphanie liked to go places on foot. For years she had lived "behind the hospital." A stranger to Paris would not understand the expression "behind the hospital," because the Salpêtrière had two equally important entrances on the two boulevards that ran alongside the campus: how could one be in front and the other behind? To understand, you had to assimilate the singular geometry of Paris, a city built in a circle but which has a front and a back . . . anything that is turned toward the center, toward Notre Dame Cathedral, is "in front," and anything facing the peripheral ring road is "behind." Because she lived in Chinatown, in a studio on top of an apartment block, not far from the suburbs, therefore, Stéphanie lived "behind."

To go below ground, and wedge her way onto an over-crowded train, and stew there amidst sweat and noise, and come back out to be shoved this way and that and affront an onslaught of people was already something of an adventure for her. After she had gone several times into the wrong building, because each building in the shopping complex was devoted to this or that product, she finally arrived, awestruck, in the "Women's Fashion" department.

She overcame her shyness and managed to get help from the sales girls; after a few mistakes, she came up with four outfits that resembled what she had described to Karl, and to her utmost surprise, actually suited her rather well . . .

On Wednesday morning, Stéphanie rushed into the changing room in her leather suit; her colleagues were lavish with compliments. Blushing, she put on her usual scrubs, feeling rather different, intentionally neglecting to close the top two buttons.

In the head nurse's office, Stéphanie was informed that Karl Bauer, the patient in room 221, would be taken into surgery for an eye operation.

When she saw Karl he was radiant.

"Do you realize, Stéphanie? I'm going to be able to see again at last."

Stéphanie had some trouble swallowing her saliva. Let him see, okay, but see her? No doubt it would be a catastrophe, the end of the dream, the death of their relationship.

"Oh, oh, Stéphanie, do you hear me? Are you still there?"

She tried to put some cheer into her voice.

"Yes, I hear you. I will be really happy for you to get your sight back. Really happy. Happy for you."

To herself she added, "not happy for me." After that, she did her best to hide her bitterness and to go along with Karl's naïve enthusiasm.

In the afternoon at four, she went off duty just as Karl, anesthetized, was going into the operating room.

On Thursday, after a night of broken sleep, she set off, with a heavy heart, for the hospital.

It was raining.

In the early morning, Paris was noisily emerging from its drowsiness. The streets belonged to giant things that hid during the day—trucks, garbage dumpsters. Vehicles splashed her with water as she went by.

The sun shone no brighter than the moon. Beneath the throbbing bridges of the elevated railway, she walked along, managing to stay dry, mumbling, "Never mind! Whether he sees me dry or soaked, he'll be filled with dismay. No point making myself look any better." With her eye glued to the shiny pavement, she thought that from now on she would once again be inhabiting her unattractive body, a body no one liked. Her beauty had just been a flash in the pan! A picnic in the grass! Her vacation from ugliness had been too short-lived . . .

At the same time she blamed herself for her sadness. What a selfish person! Instead of thinking about him, about his happiness, she was thinking about herself. An inconsiderate lover, an ugly woman, and an unprofessional nurse: she was really piling on the flaws. Besides, she herself was nothing but a flaw.

Limp, exhausted, she went through the hospital doors, her shoulders drooping, crushed by what seemed like an irreversibly discouraging weight.

The dark corridor that led to room 221 had never seemed so long.

Outside, the rain was slashing diagonally against the windows.

When she crossed the threshold, she immediately noticed

that Karl was still wearing his bandages. When she approached him, he was startled.

"Stéphanie?"

"Yes. How do you feel?"

"I think the operation failed."

The blood rushed to her ears. She was happy: he wouldn't see her, ever! Now she was ready to devote her entire life to him, if he wanted her to. Yes, she would agree to become this man's appointed nurse, provided that, from time to time, from deep within his blindness, he spoke to her of her beauty.

In the hours that followed, she was filled with inexhaustible energy, trying to boost his morale: the energy of a woman who, after a setback, has found hope again.

For more than a week, thanks to her flawlessly positive attitude, she was a great comfort to him.

One day—it was a Wednesday—he sighed.

"Do you know the worst thing about being here, that really makes me unhappy? Not hearing women's shoes."

"Those are the rules."

"They're keeping me from getting better with their rules! It's not listening to the sound of slippers and clogs that I'll recover. I need to be treated not just like a human being but also like a man."

She was instantly afraid he would ask her, because she had the suspicion she would accept.

"Please, Stéphanie, couldn't you just, for my sake, forget the rules for a few minutes and come to me wearing women's shoes, not your work shoes?"

"But . . . but . . ."

"Would they fire you for that?"

"No . . ."

"I beg you: please give me that pleasure."

"I'll think about it."

Stéphanie did indeed think of nothing else, particularly

about which shoes she could possibly wear. If she went around in her usual tennis shoes, she wasn't about to make Karl happy.

During her break she asked her most elegant coworkers for advice, and they gave her the names of a few stores.

As most of the nurses were from Martinique, when she left the hospital Stéphanie hurried underground, took the métro, and found herself in the north of Paris, in Barbès, the capital's African neighborhood, where the shop windows overflowed with tight, sophisticated shoes, modestly priced.

She nearly went back the way she'd come more than once because it was blatantly obvious that some of the shops were intended for prostitutes: the outfits were so provocative and aggressive, with vulgar designs and flashy material.

As she had been advised, she went into the "Grand Chic Parisien," a store that hardly deserved its name, judging by the neon lights and piles of boxes, and the sagging threadbare benches on patched linoleum.

Although she was determined to buy something, she was about as eager to try on high-heeled shoes as to go sheep-herding in the wilds of Transylvania. But the shop assistant encouraged her, and she managed to find a height where she didn't wobble, and decided to buy two pairs.

"What do you think of these ones?"

Stéphanie walked back and forth with the pair in question.

"No, my husband won't like them."

"He doesn't like patent leather?"

"He's blind. I mean the sound they make . . . they sound like the shoes I had at my First Communion . . . I need a sexier sound."

Delighted, the shop assistant brought a few styles with sleek curves.

"These are good," said Stéphanie, stunned by the harmony between the sound and the appearance. "Now I just have to choose the color."

"The color is easier because that's just for you."

Encouraged by her remark, Stéphanie decided on one style that she bought in two colors, red and black. In her heart of hearts she wasn't really sure about buying the carmine pumps, because she wondered if she'd ever wear them but, that day, thanks to Karl, she experienced the joy of a little girl who dreams of going off with all her mommy's sexy clothes.

On Thursday she hid her purchases in an old sports bag and went to the hospital.

At ten minutes past ten, when she was certain there wouldn't be any doctors coming in, she whispered into Karl's ear.

"I brought my shoes."

She went back out, put her clogs in such a way that she could slip them on quickly if they were disturbed, and then she put on the black pumps.

"Time for your treatment!"

She began her work by his bed. Her pointed heels tapped vigorously on the floor, quivered when she stopped, then slipped gently.

Karl grinned from ear to ear.

"What bliss," he murmured.

Suddenly Stéphanie felt like trying the scarlet pair.

"Wait, I brought some others. Oh, they're not very different but . . ."

This time it was for herself alone that she put on the pair in crimson lambskin, and on she went with her chores, amused and a bit titillated.

Karl suddenly asked, "Is the strap narrower?"

"No."

"Can you see more of your foot? Is it more cut away?"

"No."

"Is it snakeskin?"

"No."

"Then what color are they? They wouldn't be red by any chance?"

Stéphanie confirmed they were, dumbfounded. Not only had the car accident damaged Karl's optic nerve, but he was also wearing a thick bandage over his eyes. So how . . .

Almost frightened, she hurried to the door, took off the heels, put her work shoes back on, and buried the two new pairs in her bag.

"Thank you," whispered Karl, "you spoiled me."

"How did you guess?"

"I couldn't see the difference but I could feel you, you were very different in the second pair: you didn't move the same way, your hips were swaying. I bet that's the pair you wear when you want to please Ralf. Am I right?"

"Hmm . . ."

"I adore your voice, too, you have a fruity, singing, resonant voice. It's odd, such a full voice is usually characteristic of a black woman! But I don't think you are black, are you?"

"No. But I do have a few things in common with my colleagues from Martinique."

"Yes, I can hear that too. A sturdy, wide pelvis, a goddess subtly wrapped in smooth skin."

"How did you know?"

"The way you sway on your pumps, and again, your voice. Very thin women rarely have a nice voice. As if the voice needs a layer of flesh to attain depth . . . and a wide pelvis to be well grounded, rich in harmonics . . . Isn't it said of opera singers that they have vocal weight? So if a voice has weight, so must the woman. What bliss!"

"Do you really believe this stuff you're giving me?"

"Absolutely! A voice feeds on flesh and resonance. If there is neither flesh nor the space to resonate, the voice remains dry. Like the woman. No?"

"Judging by your mistresses, the other day, I thought that you only went for thin women."

"It's a combination of circumstances: I'm a photographer by

trade, so I often work with models for my fashion shoots. But I love women so much that I love what is thin in thin women and what is ample in ample women."

As of Friday, Stéphanie again had the weekend off and was at a loss. How was she going to get through three days without him?

So she decided to do things for him: she spent several hours in a beauty salon, then she treated herself to a hairdresser, managed to get an appointment to have her nails done, and then once she was back in her studio, she opened her wardrobe to have a strict look at her clothing.

"What would he like? What couldn't he like? I'm going to make two piles."

She forced herself not to cheat, emptied out her shelves and on Saturday dropped several bags off outside the offices of the Red Cross.

On Sunday she decided to go back to Barbès in order to fill her empty wardrobe and think about what Karl had explained about curvy women. If he liked them, she should manage to do the same. Sitting in a sidewalk café, she watched people come and go.

What a contrast between Barbès and Chinatown! Such a distance from her neighborhood! From the Asian streets to the African streets, everything changed, not only the smells—the green and yellow smells of Chinatown, a mixture of herbs and roots, were replaced by the scarlet, spicy, demanding smells in Barbès, of roasted lamb or grilled merguez—and the life on the street—sidewalks overflowing in Barbès and deserted streets in Chinatown; but the women as well . . . The women differed in size, allure, clothing and above all in their very concept of femininity. The Barbès women emphasized their shape by wearing lycra or enhanced it with gorgeous *boubous*, loose and colorful; while the women in Chinatown disappeared into floppy jackets, hiding any suggestion of breasts beneath a straight, mannish row of buttons, or any trace of their hips and thighs in dull trousers.

The majestic African women were regal in their loose dresses or clinging tights; they swayed to and fro beneath warm male gazes. Not for one second did they question their powers of seduction. Not for one second would they view a wolf whistle or a wink as mocking. They walked along displaying composure, insolence, and guts, so sure of their irresistible charm that they came out winners every time. Like the men around her, Stéphanie thought they were gorgeous.

She mused that if her mother were sitting there beside her at that moment, Léa would sigh as if someone were inflicting a tank parade upon her, or a visit to an institute for the handicapped, or a ballet of whales. Stephane realized that her self-disparaging attitude came from her narcissistic mother, who was a self-proclaimed standard of beauty. And it hadn't helped matters that she had left Léa to move into the Chinese neighborhood, only to find herself surrounded by tiny, ravishing models, who merely exacerbated her complex.

A scrawny, anemic redhead went by: she even looked like Léa. Stéphanie sniggered: a firefly among the marmots, that was all! Here, among these giant women, such thinness became dryness; a flat stomach meant bones showing through.

Stéphanie concluded that notions of attraction were profoundly relative; thus, greatly heartened, she went home, humming. As she was walking along the Avenue de Choisy, between the Tang supermarket and the Maison du Canard Laqué, she suddenly concluded that, after all, given her height and her glow, she must be perfectly magnificent.

Standing in front of her full-length mirror she contemplated a new woman. Her reflection had changed only slightly—her clothes, hairstyle, attitude—but an inner light—confidence—had changed her, made her a pretty, curvaceous girl with a generous bosom. She had Karl to thank for that, and she waited eagerly for the next day.

When on Monday she went through the door of room 221, the doctors' presence irritated her: it was all she could do not to chase them out the way she'd chased out the mistress, so that she could be alone with Karl; but then the nature of their gathering rang an alarm bell. Stéphanie slipped into the room, pressed up against the wall behind the interns, and adopted the modest attitude appropriate for a nurse.

With his hairy forearms and his paper mask below his chin, Dr. Belfort was worried. After a few consultations in a hushed voice with his assistants, he led the team into the meeting room to discuss the situation because, like several of the top doctors at the Salpêtrière, he felt more at ease with illnesses than with patients.

Stéphanie followed the group. As they began to go over the test results, Stéphanie learned, aghast, just how serious Karl's condition was. After several weeks, the doctors' vital prognosis remained just as cautious, if not more so, as when he was taken from the ambulance. All their hopes rested on the operations that Dr. Belfort planned to perform soon.

Stéphanie felt not only dejected but ashamed. In that room 221 where she had been running every day to live the most magical moments of her life, Karl was living the worst moments of his, perhaps the last. Lying inert in his bed, his body hooked up to rubber tubes and pouches of liquid, all alone in a tiny room at the mercy of the interns or medical students who were analyzing and commenting, he didn't own anything anymore, he didn't do anything anymore, he wasn't experiencing anything, and he was only surviving through the help of technology. She deeply resented her own selfishness; she was a monster, as childish, vain, and flirtatious as Karl's mistresses.

Consequently, that day, to punish herself, she refrained from going to visit him, and arranged for someone else to take over his treatment.

On Tuesday, when she went back to see Karl, she found him very weak. Was he asleep? She went closer, leaned over his face, but his nostrils did not react. She eventually murmured, "Karl, it's Stéphanie."

"Ah, at last . . ."

His voice came from somewhere deep inside his body, trembling with emotion. Her presence seemed to affect him.

"Four days without you, that's too long."

Although he was blind, he turned toward her.

"I haven't stopped thinking about you. I was waiting for you."

"Every day?"

"Every hour."

He was speaking gravely, without lying. She began to cry.

"Forgive me. I won't go away again."

"Thank you."

She knew that such an absurd dialogue was anything but professional: she shouldn't make such promises, and a patient does not have the right to demand them. And yet this bizarre episode enabled her to gauge the affection between them. While you couldn't say that they loved one another, you might at least suppose that they needed each other.

"Do something kind for me, Stéphanie."

"Yes, Karl, what do you want?"

"Take a mirror and describe your eyes to me."

What a bad idea, she thought regretfully, I have such ordinary brown eyes. What a pity he couldn't ask her mother on the other hand; she was so proud of her blue eyes.

Stéphanie went to get a round enlarging mirror and sat by the side of the bed, looking at her reflection.

"The whites of my eyeballs are very white."

"Like the whites of an egg?"

"Enamel white; they look deep, consistent, like cream that's been solidified in the oven."

"Good. And then?"

"A black setting, with a slight twist, sets off the iris and exalts the nuances of color."

"Ah . . . tell me about it."

"There's brown, bistre, beige, fauve, red, sometimes a hint of green. It's much more varied than you'd think."

"God is in the details. Your pupils?"

"Very black, very sensitive. They become round, and retract, freeze, and expand. My pupils are very talkative, very emotional."

"Fabulous . . . your eyelids, now."

The game went on. Eyelashes, brows, scalp, earlobes . . . Guided by a blind man's gaze, Stéphanie discovered the infinite nuances of the visible world, the unsuspected treasures of her body.

In the changing room, before leaving, she noticed outside her locker a bouquet of pink and purple peonies, set in an elegant foliage, paler than celadon. She picked it up to take it to the reception, never imagining for one second that it might be for her, when a card fell out, and on it was written, in carefully inscribed letters: "For Stéphanie, the most marvelous nurse."

Who was sending her this tribute? She searched the tissue paper wrapping, gently felt the flowers, explored the stems, in vain: she found neither signature nor clue.

Back at home, she put her present next to her bed so she could gaze at it, convinced it came from Karl.

The next morning, a new bouquet—still peonies, but yellow and red this time—was waiting for her at dawn outside her locker. The same gallant message. The same discretion on the part of the sender.

She went immediately up to room 221 and, during her conversation with Karl, she tried to verify whether he was indeed her generous purveyor. As she was unable to obtain any clues, she came right out with it: "Are you the one I have to thank for the bouquets yesterday and today?"

"I'm sorry not to have thought of it. No, it wasn't me."

"Do you swear?"

"To my great shame."

"But then who?"

"What? You have no idea who your admirer is?"

"Not the slightest idea."

"Women are insane! It takes forever to get them to open their eyes and see us. Fortunately for men, nature invented flowers . . ."

Stéphanie sulked, more out of sorts than enchanted, particularly as the gifts continued: every day, a new floral composition was left at the foot of her locker.

As a result, she felt obliged to open her eyes and look at the men who surrounded her at the Hôpital de la Salpêtrière, and she noticed, stupefied, that a number of them flashed smiles at her.

At first, she was terrified. What? Were there so many charmers around her, so many males who looked upon her as a woman? Was it really she who had not noticed them before? Or was it that they had only begun to notice her since her adventure with Karl? In shock, almost traumatized, she hesitated between maintaining her previous attitude—walking with her head down, avoiding people's gazes, withholding her smile—and adopting her new warm, relaxed attitude, where she made eye contact any number of times wherever she went, offering a dozen opportunities to stop and talk.

It was in a moment like this that she first saw Raphaël among a group of stretcher-bearers. It was hard to say exactly what it was that struck her to begin with: the young man's blazing eyes, or the peony he wore pinned to his white coat. Stéphanie shivered and realized it was a sign, and that she had just met her anonymous admirer.

She walked more slowly, batted her eyelids, opened her mouth, hunted for a sentence that didn't come, began to doubt, thought she must be wrong after all, then hurried and rushed away.

However, she ran into Raphaël again in the company of his colleagues; every time, she felt she was burning up as they looked at each other.

What could she do? How should she behave? Stéphanie had even less of an idea how to react because she wasn't expecting anything from this boy: he was a nuisance. Could she go up to him and say, "Thanks, but stop now"?

Marie-Thérèse offered her opinion while they were at the cafeteria.

"That stretcher-bearer Raphaël, I think he's devouring you with his eyes, Stéphanie."

"Oh, really? He's not bad . . ."

"Are you joking? He's the cutest guy in the hospital. He has long eyelashes like an Egyptian princess. We're all crazy about him. We'll be green with envy if you hook up with him."

"Me? Why me?"

"Those flowers! Everyone knows about it, girl. He is just crazy about you."

"Don't you think he's too young?"

"Too young for who? He's the same age as you."

Marie-Thérèse was right. Spontaneously, since she'd realized she could be attractive around Karl, a man of forty, Stéphanie had been considering herself to be older, classifying herself along with the fortysomethings, and initially she thought it was too bold, or even indecent, to respond to the advances of a mere youth.

The week was hectic. Stéphanie did not spend too much time with Karl; he had undergone a new operation and was easily tired; also, by chance she happened to witness his behavior with other nurses, and understood that with her he was making himself tired trying to be funny, deep, and disconcerting, and that he often made an excessive and costly effort. In addition, she dreaded walking through the floors and running into Raphaël.

The following Saturday and Sunday, although she didn't have to go to work, she did go to the hospital. She dressed up, convinced that Karl would be sensitive to how she looked, and she even went so far as to inaugurate the lace lingerie that she had just bought. However, when she saw a few of the former mistresses waiting in the lobby, she turned around and headed back the way she'd come, swapped her Indian silk blouse and jersey skirt for her regulation scrubs, then went back upstairs as a nurse.

Her colleagues were astonished to see her there, so she explained that she was doing overtime in ophthalmology, in the ward across the way, and then she seized a moment when they weren't paying attention to slip into room 221. The last mistress had just left, and Karl gave her some time.

"Have you noticed? I have fewer visitors as the weeks go by. They only appreciated me when I was in good health—strong, funny, somebody who made them feel good."

"Are you angry with them?"

"No. It's probably because that's the way they are—voracious, eager to charm, to conquer, to live—that I liked them to begin with."

"How many came back?"

"Two. There'll only be one left next week. They have finally managed to get along, these women who hate each other; they've arranged to take turns getting news about me by coming here as little as possible. It's funny, no? Basically, they're impatient, in a hurry to weep for me, they'll be dazzling at my funeral. And sincere. Yes, I mean it, really."

"Don't say that, you'll get better! We're going to fight together to get you back on your feet."

"My mistresses don't believe that . . ."

"I don't even want to make fun of them. It must not have been hard to fall in love with you: you're so handsome."

"Male beauty is useless. What makes for a man's attraction is not his beauty, but the way he convinces a woman that she is beautiful in his presence."

"Blah blah blah!"

"Useless, I assure you. Physical perfection gets in the way, it's a handicap."

"Go on!"

"Okay, listen: the fact you think I'm decorative—what does that inspire in you? Trust or wariness?"

"It inspires desire."

"Thank you. Now, be honest: trust or wariness?"

"Wariness."

"You see! The first thing people are wary of—they assume that handsome men are not sincere. The second thing: handsome men inspire jealousy. I've only ever known jealous women."

"Were they wrong?"

"The first time they threw a jealous fit, yes. After that, no. Since their suspicion preceded my acts, I felt obliged to prove them right."

They laughed, relaxed.

"Let me explain, Stéphanie, why one must never be jealous. Because if you create a unique relationship with someone, it will not be reproduced. For example, in this very moment, do you think I could have this discussion with another woman?"

"No."

"So you must consider, Stéphanie, that with me you have no rivals."

She smiled and then brought her lips closer to his to whisper, "Yes I do."

He shivered.

"Who?"

"Death. One day death can take away this unique thing I am living with you."

"And so you hate death?"

"Why am I a nurse? Why do you think I am looking after you so well? I will help you to get better."

They stayed in silence for a long while, very close to each other, sharing the same emotion. Then Stéphanie kissed him furtively and rushed out.

On Monday morning in the changing room, it wasn't a bouquet waiting for Stéphanie, but Raphaël.

Intimidated, with the burning boldness of shy people in his eyes, he quickly handed her a spray of roses.

"Hi, I'm Raphaël."

"I know."

"I'm the one who . . . since . . . well . . . you understand . . ."

"Yes, I know that, too."

She suggested they sit down on the bench next to the long sink.

The stretcher bearer murmured, as if he were in ecstasy, "You are beautiful."

On hearing him, Stéphanie realized that she had left the world of the blind behind; this was a sighted man who was saying this, a sighted man with his eyes wide open.

"Raphaël, I'm not free."

The young man's face fell, instantly devastated by pain.

"That can't be," he murmured.

"I'm afraid so, I'm not free."

"Are you going to get married?"

Amazed by the concrete nature of the question, Stéphanie replied in a toneless voice.

"Perhaps. Nothing is planned. I . . . I love him. It's . . . it's like a disease."

Stéphanie almost confessed that Karl was sick then, at the last minute, out of caution, she turned the phrase around on herself, so her colleague would not suspect anything. She insisted, "You see, my feelings . . . it's like a sickness. I don't know when I'll get better, or even if I will get better."

He reflected. Then he looked into her eyes.

"Stéphanie, I realize that I'm not the only man who's interested in you, I realize that I have rivals, and I realize that the world is full of men who would like to live with you. However, with my flowers, I was coming to ask you if I was in with a chance, even a tiny chance."

Stéphanie thought about the doctors' cautious diagnoses, and the anxiety she felt every morning going into the room where Karl lay, so weak . . . Unable to continue the conversation, she burst into tears.

Disconcerted, Raphaël wriggled from one buttock to the other, muttering Stéphanie's name, hunting around to see what he could come up with to check the deluge of tears. Awkwardly, he put his arm around her shoulders, and encouraged her to lean against him. As she was sobbing, he smiled, because for the first time he got a whiff of her scent, and it made him giddy. Stéphanie, slumped against his chest, discovered that, while most stretcher-bearers smelled of stale tobacco, this boy had incredibly soft skin that gave off a heady perfume of hazelnut. Confused, she sat up. Trying to get a hold of herself, she remembered the operations Dr. Belfort had talked about, and she pictured herself helping Karl to sit up, to take his first steps . . . She shook her head, looked her admirer in the eye, and said, "Forget about me."

"You don't fancy me?"

"Never, do you hear me, Raphaël: never!"

When she went through the door of room 221, she unbuttoned the top of her blouse and saw Karl looking even paler, emaciated. As usual, he did not let his worries show through.

With a brisk movement she slid the bedpan under the sheets, and hardly recognized his legs: his thighs and calves had melted away. She was eager for Dr. Belfort to begin these vital operations.

"What's up, Stéphanie, you don't talk about Ralf anymore."

"It's over."

"So much the better, he was a jerk. So who's your new boyfriend?"

Stéphanie felt like shouting, "You, you idiot, I love only you, there is no one as important as you," but she knew that would not be in keeping with their relationship, for he thought that she was independent, fulfilled, happy. And so she answered, "Raphaël."

"He's a lucky guy, that Raphaël! Does he know it?"

Stéphanie thought back on the episode she had just experienced and declared, "Yes. He does."

Karl registered the information at face value.

"So much the better. I want you to promise me one thing, Stéphanie, will you?"

"Yes."

"Lend me your ear: I can only whisper this kind of request, and that way I can enjoy the way you smell better."

Stéphanie put her ear up against Karl's well-defined lips, listened attentively to his murmur. As soon as he had finished, she protested, "No! I won't! Don't even talk like that!"

He insisted. She put her ear back against his lips, then with tears flowing from her eyes, she agreed.

The medical team performed the decisive operation. Going round in circles outside the security door, Stéphanie, who was not religious, implored the heavens to make it a success. Dr. Belfort came out of the operating room rubbing his hands, looking pleased. Stéphanie clung to this detail to keep her faith.

Then, in the space of four days Karl's condition deteriorated. He went into a coma during the night and, on the morning of the fifth day, the doctors began to doubt whether they'd be able to revive him. Stéphanie clenched her teeth, trying to hide how distraught she felt, battling with her colleagues to chase death away from where it was lurking in room 221.

At the end of the afternoon, she had to go to the distant infirmary at the other end of the compound.

The sky was a springtime blue, sharp and cloudless. The brisk air filled her lungs. Birds were chirping as if to announce a joyful event.

A bell rang out on the half hour.

Stéphanie found herself hoping: she hurried her steps to return to reanimation.

When she went through the security doors, she sensed that something was going on.

At the end of the corridor, banging the door to his room, the nurses' aides were busily moving about.

She broke into a run and went through the door.

Karl had just died.

She leaned her back against the wall and slid slowly to the ground. There she stayed, her legs spread, without saying a word, without a cry, her eyes overflowing with tears.

Her colleagues looked at her disapprovingly: a professional must never give in to emotion, otherwise it becomes impossible to do one's job.

Overwhelmed, she suddenly remembered Karl's whispered words: her promise.

She jumped to her feet, ran down the corridor, drying her eyes, down to the ground floor, on to the emergency unit, then straight up to where Raphaël was standing smoking with the other stretcher-bearers.

"Have you finished your shift?"

"In ten minutes."

"Then let's leave together. Let's go to your place."

Dumbfounded, he hesitated. She misunderstood his hesitation and insisted: "It's now or never!"

"Then it's now!" exclaimed Raphaël, tossing his cigarette away.

He took her by the hand and led her back to the changing room. On the way, she felt the need to explain herself: "You see, I'm coming with you because . . . because . . ."

"I get it. You're all better?"

"That's it. I'm all better."

One hour after Karl's death, Stéphanie, loyal to her promise, gave herself to Raphaël. She made love with passion and rage. Not for a moment did Raphaël suspect she was a virgin. But when she let the young man embrace her, although it was to Raphaël that she parted her legs, it was for Karl that she said, "I love you."

TRASHY READING

"Me, read novels? Never!"

Although he lived surrounded by thousands of books, boards sagging wearily from floor to ceiling along the walls of his gloomy apartment, he became indignant at the mere suggestion that he might possibly waste his time with fiction.

"The facts, nothing but the facts! Facts, and ideas. Until the day I run out of reality, I will not grant a single second to unreality."

Very few people entered Maurice Plisson's apartment, because he didn't like having people around; however, from time to time, when one of his students showed a real spark of interest for his discipline, he would gratify him at the end of the school year with a reward, a privileged moment: an hour with his teacher over a mug of beer, served with a handful of peanuts on the coffee table of his living room. Every time, the student—shoulders sloping, knees close together, intimidated by the premises—would gaze at all the shelves and see that filling all that space were essays, studies, biographies, and encyclopedias, but not a single book of literature.

"Do you not like novels, Monsieur Plisson?"

"You might as well ask me if I like lying."

"To that degree?"

"Look, my young friend, from the moment I first realized my passion for history, geography, and law, despite forty-five years of assiduous reading at the rate of several books a week, I am still learning. What could I possibly discover in a novel, a work of mere fantasy? No, tell me: what? If they tell a true story, I already know it; and if they make something up, I couldn't care less."

"But literature . . ."

"I don't want to belittle my colleagues, or dampen your energy, particularly as you are a brilliant student and quite capable of admission to the École normale supérieure, but, if I am to be perfectly frank, I will say: stop boring us with literature! Stuff and nonsense! Reading novels is an occupation for a woman on her own—although knitting or embroidery would be more useful. Those who write novels are writing for a population of idle women, no one else, and they're seeking votes. Wasn't it Paul Valéry, a respectable intellectual, who refused to write a text which began with 'The marquise went out at five o'clock?' He was absolutely right! If he refused to write it, I refuse to read it: 'The Marquise went out at five o'clock!' First of all, the marquise of what? Where does she live? In what era? Who can prove to me that it was truly five o'clock, not five ten or five thirty? And besides, what would that change, if it was ten o'clock in the morning or ten o'clock at night, since it's all made up? You see, novels reflect the reign of the arbitrary, complete vagueness. I'm a serious man. I don't have the place, or the time, or the energy to devote to such nonsense."

He felt that his arguments were irrefutable, and this year as in all other years, they produced an identical effect: the student did not reply. Maurice Plisson had won.

If he had been able to hear his student's thoughts, he would have found out that silence did not mean victory. Disturbed by his peremptory tone, considering his theory to be too cut and dried for an intelligent man, the young man wondered why his professor kept such a distance from the imaginary, and why he was so wary of art and emotion; and what surprised him most of all was his professor's scorn regarding "women on their own," since it came from a man on his own. For it was public knowledge at the Lycée du Parc that Monsieur Plisson was a "confirmed old bachelor," and had never been seen in the company of a woman.

Maurice Plisson offered his student another bottle of beer, as a way of signaling the end of the interview. The student understood, mumbled some thanks, and followed his professor to the door.

"Have a good vacation, young man. And just remember that it would be a very good idea if you were to begin revising your ancient history already in August, because in the course of the coming year, you won't really have time before the entrance exams."

"I'll do that, sir. Greek and Latin history as of August 1st, I'll follow your advice. My parents will have to agree to take a trunk full of books with us on vacation."

"Where will you be?"

"In Provence, where my family has an estate. And you?"

While the student may have asked his question simply to be polite, it nevertheless surprised Maurice Plisson. He squinted his eyelids and looked for help in the distance.

"Well . . . we . . . in the Ardèche, this year."

"I love the Ardèche. Whereabouts?"

"But . . . but . . . listen, I don't know, it's . . . a friend who is renting a house. Ordinarily, we go on package tours, but this summer, we will have a real stay in the Ardèche. She decided for us, she took care of everything and . . . I don't remember the name of the village."

The student maintained a kindly attitude toward his professor's embarrassment, shook his hand, and went down the steps four at a time, impatient to meet up with his friends and spread the news of the day: Plisson had a girlfriend! All the gossipmongers had been wrong about him, those who thought he was a homosexual, or those who said he visited

prostitutes, or the ones who believed he was still a virgin . . .
In truth, Plisson, although he was ugly, had had a woman in
his life for years, a woman with whom he traveled around the
world, whom he met up with during the breaks, and, who
knows, maybe even every Friday evening. Why didn't they
live together? Two possible explanations. Either she lived far
away . . . or she was married. Good old Plisson, he would be
the main topic of conversation that summer, among the students in the final year.

When he had closed the door behind his student, the professor could have kicked himself. Why had he spoken? Never,
in the thirty years of his career, had he given away the slightest
clue about his private life. How could he have yielded? It was
because of that question, "Where, in Ardèche?" and he realized
that he had forgotten . . . With his memory like an elephant, he
usually remembered everything . . . It was so distressing that,
consequently, wanting to make up for his slip, he had mentioned Sylvie . . .

What had he said? Oh, it hardly mattered . . . Dreaded ail-
ments usually started like this, with confusion, or a lapse, a
memory that escaped you . . . Now his brain was boiling. He
must have a fever! Was that the second symptom? Could your
brain degenerate that quickly?

He dialed Sylvie's number, and while it was ringing, because
she didn't usually take so long to answer, he suddenly became
afraid he'd dialed the wrong number without realizing . . .

"It's even worse than I thought. If I mixed up the numbers,
and if someone else starts talking to me, I'll hang up and head
straight to the hospital."

After the tenth ring, a voice answered, sounding very surprised: "Yes?"

"Sylvie?" he asked, breathless, in a dull voice.

"Yes."

He took a breath: it wasn't so bad, at least he had dialed the correct number.

"It's Maurice."

"Oh, forgive me, Maurice, I didn't recognize you. I was at the back of the apartment . . . what's going on? You don't usually call me at this time?"

"Sylvie, where is it we are going this summer, in the Ardèche?"

"To a friend's house . . . well, a friend of friends . . ."

"What's the place called?"

"I have no idea."

Appalled, Maurice fluttered his eyelids, tensed his fingers on the receiver: Sylvie, too! We are both suffering from it.

"Would you believe that I couldn't remember the name you had given me either," squealed Maurice, "when a student asked me."

"Maurice, I don't see how you could have repeated something I never told you. This friend . . . or rather, friend of friends . . . in short, the landlady drew me a map to get there because the property is in an isolated rural area, far from any village."

"Really? You didn't tell me anything?"

"No."

"Are you sure?"

"Yes."

"So I didn't forget anything? So everything is okay?" exclaimed Maurice.

"Hang on a second," she said, without suspecting how greatly she had relieved his anxiety, "I'll go get the paper and answer your question."

Maurice Plisson collapsed in the Voltaire armchair he had inherited from a great-aunt, and smiled to his apartment, which suddenly seemed to him as beautiful as the château of Versailles. Saved! Rescued! Safe and sound! No, he was not about to depart from his beloved books just yet, his brain was still functioning, Alzheimer's disease was camped outside, well beyond the fortress wall of his meninges. Begone, threats and fantasies!

From the crackling sound in the headset, he guessed that Sylvie was going through her papers; finally, he heard a victory cry.

"Here, I've got it. Are you still there, Maurice?"

"Yes."

"We will be in the gorges of the Ardèche, in a house built at the end of a road that has no name. Let me explain: after the village of Saint-Martin-des-Fossés, you take the road to Châtaigniers; there, on the third road after the crossroads with a statue of the Virgin Mary, you drive for two kilometers. Is that a good enough answer?"

"It's fine."

"Do you want to have your mail forwarded?"

"For two weeks it's not worth it."

"Me neither. Especially with such an address."

"Okay, Sylvie, I don't want to keep you any longer. As you know, the telephone and I . . . See you on Saturday, then?"

"Saturday, ten o'clock."

In the days that followed, Maurice dined out on the cheerfulness which had closed this conversation: not only was he in fine form, but he was also about to leave on vacation!

Like many single people who have no sexual life, he worried a great deal about his health. The moment anyone mentioned an illness in his presence, Maurice imagined he would catch it and from that very moment he lay in wait for it to show up. The more the illness revealed itself through vague, uncharacteristic symptoms, such as fatigue, headaches, sweating, and gastric discomfort, the more he dreaded he was infected. His doctor, just as he was about to close his office, would see Plisson show up, looking feverish, hands trembling, mouth dry, desperate to obtain confirmation of his imminent demise. Every time, the physician conducted an in-depth examination—or at least gave his patient that impression—before going on to reassure him and send him home as delighted as if he had been cured of a real ailment.

On those evenings, when he felt he had been set free, as if he had been granted clemency on death row, Maurice Plisson would get undressed and look with satisfaction at his reflection in the full-length mirror in his bedroom—a relic from his grandmother, a solid burr walnut wardrobe with an inside mirror. To be sure, he was not handsome, and no more handsome than before, but he was healthy. Entirely healthy. And this body that nobody wanted—it was purer than many attractive bodies, and would live even longer. On those evenings, Maurice Plisson liked himself. Without the intense fears with which he periodically inoculated himself, he might have been incapable of displaying such affection toward himself. Besides, who else would have shown it to him?

On Saturday at ten o'clock he blew his horn outside the building where they had arranged to meet.

Sylvie came out on the balcony, fat, giggling, badly dressed.

"Hey there, cousin!"

"Hey, cousin!"

Sylvie and Maurice had been friends since childhood. When they were young, and he was an only son, and she was an only daughter, they had adored each other so much that they had promised to marry when they grew up. Alas, an uncle who had been let in on their secret explained to them that first cousins were not allowed to get married, which put an end to their matrimonial projects, but not their friendship. Was it the shadow of their doomed nuptials that prevented them from creating lasting ties with others? Did they never resolve to envisage any other relationship, after that original one? And now they were both fifty years of age, with doomed love affairs behind them, and they were resigned to their single status. They spent time together the way they used to, during vacation, with as much if not more pleasure, because each time they met it was as if they were annihilating time and the hardship of life. Every year, they gave each other two weeks, and they had been together to Egypt, Italy, Greece, Turkey, Syria, Lebanon, and Russia, for Maurice appreciated cultural trips. And Sylvie liked traveling of any kind.

In a whirlwind of veils and shawls that floated around her enormous body, she came out the front door of her building, glanced over at Maurice, and strode across the sidewalk to the garage to load another suitcase into her tiny car. Maurice wondered why this obese woman systematically bought tiny cars. Not only did they make her seem more voluminous, they could not be very practical in the long run.

"Well, Maurice, what are you thinking?"

She went up to him and gave him a resounding kiss.

Crushed against her monumental bosom, trying on the tip of his toes to reach a cheek where he could leave a kiss, he suddenly saw himself as if he were Sylvie's car. Puny, hollow-chested, short, with slender joints, on a photo next to Sylvie and her Mini he would have looked as if he belonged to her collection.

"I was looking around the parking lot and I remembered that on my street there are two blacks who have white limousines. Black. White. The opposite. Have you noticed?"

She burst out laughing.

"No, but you reminded me that one of my colleagues at the town hall, Madame N'Da, has a bichon, a cream colored dog, that she's crazy about."

Maurice was going to smile when he noticed to his horror that his car—long, high, solid, with a body of American proportions—confirmed the law of opposites. He would never have suspected that he too was trying to compensate for his own complexes through the choice of his automobile.

"Maurice, you seem somewhat tired . . ."

"No, everything is fine. We've been talking on the phone for months without seeing each other, so how are you?"

"Just great! I'm always just great, Maurice!"

"Did you do something with your hair?"

"Oh, hardly . . . what do you think? Is it better?"

"Yes, it's better," replied Maurice, not really sure what he thought.

"You might also have noticed that I lost ten pounds—but nobody notices that."

"Actually, I was wondering . . ."

"Liar! And in any case, it's ten pounds off my brain that I've lost, not ten pounds of fat. So those ten pounds, you won't see them, you can just hear them!"

She gave a deep, full-throated laugh.

Although he didn't laugh with her, Maurice nevertheless looked at her indulgently. Over time, his affection had been tempered with lucidity: he knew that his cousin was very different from him—not terribly cultured, too sociable, fond of gargantuan meals, dirty jokes, and fun-loving loudmouths, but he didn't hold it against her; as she was the only person that he loved, he had decided to like her too, that is, to take her as she was. Even the pity he felt toward her unattractive physique—increasingly unattractive with each passing year—reinforced his tenderness. Basically, the compassion he showed Sylvie for her lack of physical charm was in lieu of the one he could have shown himself.

Leaving Lyon and its winding freeway overpasses behind, they drove in convoy for several hours. As they drew closer to the south, the heat seemed to change consistency: thick, paralyzing, and motionless in the region around Lyon, like a lead shield burning above mortal beings, it gradually became airier, with a pleasant breeze as they followed the Rhône River, then it became drier and somehow mineral when they reached the Ardèche.

In the middle of the afternoon, after making mistakes that added to Sylvie's good mood, they managed to find the wild dusty road that took them to the villa.

Maurice immediately noticed that the qualities of the place might also be its defects: clinging to a rocky slope where only a few thirsty bushes survived, the house, of natural stone as ocher as the surrounding countryside, was situated miles from the nearest village, and several hundred yards from the nearest neighbor.

"Excellent," he exclaimed, to win Sylvie's approval, for she looked doubtful; "a perfect place to rest!"

She smiled and decided to share his opinion.

Once they had chosen their rooms and unpacked their belongings—books for Maurice—Sylvie made sure the television and radio were working, then offered to go and stock up on supplies in the nearest supermarket.

Maurice went with her because, knowing his cousin's temperament, he was afraid she would buy too much and spend too much.

Pushing the shopping cart, he went along the aisles with Sylvie who wanted to buy everything, babbling, comparing products with the ones she found at home, and criticizing the selection. Once the most dangerous part had been taken care of—preventing Sylvie from emptying the entire cold meats department into her shopping cart—they headed for the checkout counter.

"Stay there, I'm going to get a book!" exclaimed Sylvie.

Maurice mastered his irritation because he wanted his vacation to be a successful one; mentally, however, he placed his unfortunate cousin before the firing squad. Buying a book in the supermarket! Had he ever, even once in his life, bought a book in a supermarket? A book was a sacred, precious object, one you first read about on the bibliographical list, and then you went on to find out more about it, and only then, if you really wanted to, did you write the reference on a piece of paper and go to order it from a bookseller worthy of the name. Under no circumstances should a book ever be selected from among the sausages, vegetables, and washing powders.

"What a sad time we live in . . ." he murmured through his lips.

Unabashedly, Sylvie pranced around among the piles and shelves of books as if they were appetizing. With a quick glance, Maurice confirmed that naturally the supermarket sold nothing but novels and, feeling like a martyr, he glued his eyes to the ceiling while he waited for Sylvie to finish sniffing this cover, or inhaling that volume, or feeling the weight of this one, or leafing through pages as if she were checking whether there was dirt in the salad.

Suddenly, she gave out a cry.

"Way cool! The latest Chris Black!"

Maurice had no idea who this Chris Black was, to be triggering a pre-orgasmic state in his cousin, and he did not deign to pay the slightest attention to the volume she threw onto the pile of shopping in the cart.

"You've never read any Chris Black? It's true, you don't read novels. Listen, it's great. You can devour it in one sitting, you are, like, drooling on every page, you can't put it down until you've finished it."

Maurice noticed that Sylvie talked about the book as if it were something to eat.

"I suppose they're right, the salespeople, to put the books in with the food," he thought, "because for this type of consumers, it's exactly the same thing."

"Listen, Maurice, if you want to do me a favor someday, read some Chris Black."

"Listen, Sylvie, just to please you, I can put up with you talking to me about this Chris Black, whom I don't know from Adam, and that's already a great deal. Just don't count on me to read him."

"It's really stupid, you'll die without knowing what you've missed."

"I don't think so. And if I do die, it won't be because of that."

"Oh, you must think I have bad taste . . . and yet, when I read Chris Black, I'm perfectly aware I'm not reading Marcel Proust, I'm not that stupid."

"Why? Have you read Marcel Proust?"

"Now you're being mean, Maurice. No, you know perfectly well I haven't read Marcel Proust, unlike yourself."

Like some Saint Blandina of culture, smarting with wounded dignity, Maurice smiled, as if he were finally being awarded a quality that had been only stingily conceded to him before. Basically, he found it delightful that, both his cousin and his students assumed he must have read Proust—something that he had never even attempted, because he was allergic to narrative literature. So much the better. He would not deny it. He had read so many other books . . . Unto those that have shall more be given, no?

"Maurice, I'm well aware that I'm not reading a great masterpiece but, on the other hand, I'm having a really good time."

"You are free, you have the right to have fun however you want, it's none of my business."

"Trust me: if you're bored, Chris Black is as great as Dan West."

He could not suppress a chuckle.

"Chris Black, Dan West—even their names are simplistic, two syllables, almost onomatopoeias, easy to remember. Any idiot chewing gum in Texas could repeat them absolutely flawlessly. Do you think those are their real names or do they rename them to apply the laws of marketing?"

"What do you mean?"

"I mean, Chris Black or Dan West, that's easier to read on an end display than Jules Michelet."

Sylvie was about to reply when suddenly she gave a shout on seeing some friends. Wiggling her chubby fingers, she pounced on three women who were as imposing as she was.

Maurice felt piqued. Sylvie would abandon him for a good half an hour now, the minimum length of time for a short conversation by her standards.

From a distance, he gave a faint wave to Sylvie's friends, just to emphasize that he wouldn't be joining in their improvised meeting; he would simply have to grin and bear it while he waited. With his elbows on the edge of the shopping cart, he let his gaze wander over the products for sale. The cover of the book gave him pause. How vulgar! Black, red, gold, puffy letters, an exaggerated expressionistic design that sought to give the impression that the book contained terrible things, as if they had put a label on it to warn the reader, "Caution, poison!" or "Do not touch, high voltage, danger of death." And the title— *The Chamber of Dark Secrets*—it would be hard to find anything more trivial, wouldn't it? Gothic and contemporary, two forms of bad taste under one cover! Moreover, as if the title were not already enough, the publisher had added this blurb: "When you close this book, you won't leave fear behind!" How ghastly . . . No need to open the book to know it was absolute shit.

Chris Black . . . He'd rather die than read a book by Chris Black! On top of it, it was corpulent, hefty—like Sylvie herself, actually; it was supposed to give you your money's worth.

Making sure that Sylvie and her friends, absorbed by their conversation, weren't looking at him, he discreetly turned the book over. How many pages were there in this door stop? Eight hundred pages! How awful! When I think they cut trees down for this, to print the unspeakable garbage of Mr. Chris Black . . .

He must sell millions of volumes all over the world, the bastard . . . For each of his bestsellers they must destroy a three-hundred-year-old forest, slash, down it comes, the sap flows! This is why the planet is being trashed, why the earth's lungs are disappearing, its reserves of oxygen, its ecosystems—so that fat women can read fat books that are worthless trash! It disgusts me . . .

Since the women were still chatting without paying him the slightest attention, he leaned closer to read the back cover.

If she had known where the adventure would take her, FBI agent Eva Simplon would never have lingered at Darkwell House. But she has just inherited it from a distant aunt, and needs to stay the time it takes to arrange the sale. Should she have refused such a poisoned gift? In store for her are some surprises as mysterious as they are hair-raising . . .

Who is meeting after midnight in an inaccessible room deep in the house, with no apparent entrance? Whose are these voices chanting in the night? And who are these strange buyers offering millions of dollars for an isolated old house?

And the 16th century manuscript her aunt told her about one day—what is so explosive about it to make so many people covet it?

Agent Eva Simplon has her work cut out for her, and the reader is in danger of losing sleep along with her.

Aw, isn't that cute . . . so idiotic that you can already see the film—Maurice Plisson also hated the cinema—with shrieking violins, blue lightning, and a ditzy blonde running through the darkness . . . What was fascinating was not so much that there were imbeciles prepared to read this pap, but that there was someone unfortunate enough to write it. There are no stupid professions; however, one could aim for a less unworthy way of paying one's rent. Moreover, it must take months to churn out eight hundred pages. There are two explanations possible: either this Chris Black is a swine infatuated with his own talent, or he's a slave to a publisher who stands there with a pistol up against his forehead. "Eight hundred pages, buddy, and not a page less!" "Why eight hundred, sir?" "Because, you dummy, you shit-faced scribbler, the average American can only donate $20 of his monthly budget and thirty-five hours of his monthly time to reading, so you give me a book worth $20 and thirty-five hours of reading, okay? No need to go over, no more, no less. It's good value for money, the law of the marketplace. Got it? And stop quoting Dostoyevsky to me, I hate communists."

Leaning on his shopping cart, his shoulders shaking with sarcastic mirth, Maurice Plisson delighted in inventing the scene. Good old Chris Black, you had to feel sorry for him, in the end.

And then what he had been afraid of happened: Sylvie insisted on introducing him to her friends.

"Come here, Maurice, it's through them that I found the rental. Grace, Audrey, and Sofia are staying not far from us, two miles away. We'll have a chance to meet again."

Maurice stammered a few words that must have seemed friendly enough, while wondering if Parliament shouldn't draft a bill to outlaw giving the names of beautiful women—Grace, Audrey, Sofia—to fatties. Then there were promises of meeting for orange juice, or petanque games, or walks in the country, and they parted with emphatic assurances of meeting up again soon.

As they drove back to the Villa, with a deserted countryside flashing by the window, Maurice could not help but think about *The Chamber of Dark Secrets*—what a ridiculous title—because there was one detail that had captured his curiosity. Which 16th century manuscript could it be that the plot revolved around? It had to be a work that existed, American novelists lack imagination, according to his literary colleagues. A treatise on alchemy? A memoir of the Templars? A register with inadmissible family trees? A text by Aristotle that had been thought lost? In spite of himself, Maurice could not help but play with various hypotheses. After all, Chris Black, or whoever it was that hid behind the pseudonym, might be more than a pompous ass full of his own genius, he might be an honest researcher, an erudite, one of those brilliant academics the United States know how to produce, but who is underpaid . . . Why not someone like himself, Maurice Plisson? What if he were a decent man of letters who only accepted to write such vile porridge in order to pay his debts or feed his family? Perhaps not everything was bad in the book.

Maurice was annoyed with himself for showing such indulgence, and he decided to think about more serious subjects. And so it was almost in spite of himself that he stole the book while he was emptying the shopping from the trunk: using the pretext of a trip between the car and the pantry, within three seconds he had slipped it into a porcelain umbrella stand.

Sylvie was busy fixing up the kitchen, making the evening meal, and didn't realize. To prevent her from thinking about it, Maurice even suggested watching television, specifying however that, as was his habit, he would go to bed early.

"If I stick her in front of the box, she won't think about reading and she'll be glued to her armchair until the last weather report."

Everything went according to plan. Delighted to discover that her cousin would agree to pleasures as simple as an evening watching a movie, Sylvie declared that this would be a great vacation together, and they had been right not to go traveling this year, this would be a good change.

After half an hour of a movie he didn't watch, Maurice yawned ostentatiously and said he was going up to bed.

"Don't move, don't lower the volume, I'm so tired by the trip I'll fall asleep right away. Goodnight, Sylvie."

"Goodnight, Maurice."

As he crossed the hall, he grabbed the book from the bottom of the umbrella stand, slipped it under his shirt, hurried up to his room and raced through his washing and toothbrushing, closed the door, and settled in bed with *The Chamber of Dark Secrets.*

"I just want to find out what this 16th century manuscript is," he decided.

Twenty minutes later, he was no longer asking that question: any critical distance he had hoped to keep with regard to the text had only lasted a few pages; by the end of the first chapter, he started the next one without pausing for breath; as he read, his sarcasm melted like sugar in water.

To his great surprise, he learned that the heroine, FBI agent Eva Simplon, was a lesbian; he was so astonished that from that moment on he could no longer cast any doubt over the acts or ideas that the author ascribed to her. Moreover, because this beautiful woman's sexuality marginalized her to some degree, Maurice recognized his own feeling of marginalization—his ugliness; very quickly he felt a strong connection with Eva Simplon.

When he heard Sylvie switch off the television and clump heavily up the stairs, he was reminded that he was supposed to be sleeping. Feeling deceitful, he hastily switched off the light on the bed table. But she mustn't know that he was still up! Still less that he'd gone off with her book! And she mustn't take it back . . .

The minutes he had to spend in darkness seemed long and fretful. The house was creaking with a thousand noises too complicated to identify. Had Sylvie remembered to lock all the doors and windows? Surely not! He knew how trusting she was, by nature. Did she not realize they were living in a strange house, built in the middle of nowhere, in the wilderness? Who could guarantee that the region wasn't infested with prowlers, burglars, and unscrupulous individuals ready to kill them for a credit card? Maybe there was even a maniac on the loose who broke into villas to cut the throats of their inhabitants? A serial killer. The butcher of the Ardèche Gorges. Or even a gang . . . Clearly everyone in the area knew this except for them, the new-comers, because no one had warned them, and that made them ideal targets! He shivered.

Here was the dilemma: should he get up to go and check that everything was locked, which would show Sylvie he was still up, or let miscreants get into the house, to hide in the closet or in the cellar? At that very moment, a lugubrious sound echoed in the night.

An owl?

Yes. Bound to be.

Or a man imitating an owl to alert his accomplices? The oldest trick in the world for miscreants. No?

No! Of course it was an owl.

He heard the cry again.

Maurice began to sweat; the small of his back was soaking. What could the repetition mean? Did it prove it was a real owl or was it an answer from an accomplice?

He sat up and quickly put on his slippers. Not a minute to lose. Never mind what Sylvie might think, he was more worried about a gang of psychopaths than his cousin.

As he rushed out into the corridor, he heard the splashing of the shower; that reassured him: she wouldn't hear him going downstairs.

When he got down there, and saw the living room and dining room bathed in a spectral light, he found to his horror that she had left everything open. Not a single window shutter, nor the shutters to the French doors, had been closed; you only had to break a window to get in. As for the door, there it was with the key in the lock, not even turned. Foolish wretch! With people like her, was it any wonder that there were murders.

Hastily, he went out and, not even taking the time to breathe, so afraid was he of losing a second, he pushed closed the wooden panels, running from window to window, not daring to look at the gray countryside behind him, dreading with each instant that a hand would come down onto the back of his neck to knock him out.

Then he went back inside, turned the key, drove home the bolts, lowered the latches, and once again ran around inside to block all the shutters with their bar.

Once he'd finished his sprint, he sat down to catch his breath. As his heartbeat gradually slowed, since everything seemed calm around him, he understood that he had just suffered from a panic attack.

"What's happening, my poor Maurice? You haven't been terrified like this since childhood."

He remembered having been a fearful little boy, but he thought that he had left that sort of fragility far behind him, in a vanished world, in a Maurice who had disappeared. Could it come back?

"It must be that book! I certainly have no reason to be proud of myself."

Mumbling to himself, he went back to his room.

Just as he was about to unplug the light, he hesitated.

"A few more pages?"

If he didn't switch off the lights, and Sylvie got up again, she would see the light under her cousin's door and be surprised that he was awake, although he had claimed he couldn't keep his eyes open.

He hunted in the wardrobe for a comforter, and put it at the foot of the door to block the space, then switched the light back on and settled down to read.

This Eva Simplon certainly didn't disappoint him. She reasoned the way he did, criticized the way he did, even if she went on to suffer from her critical standards. Yes, just like him. He greatly appreciated the woman.

Two hundred pages farther along, his eyelids were struggling so hard to stay open that he decided to call it a day and go to sleep. As he was plumping his pillow to settle down, he recalled the numerous footnotes that referred to Eva Simplon's previous exploits. What bliss! He'd be able to find his heroine in other books.

Basically, Sylvie was right. It wasn't great literature, but it was fascinating. And in any case, he didn't cherish great literature either. Tomorrow he'd have to find a way to go off on his own in order to continue his reading.

He was just drifting off when a thought made him sit up on his mattress.

"Sylvie . . . of course . . ."

Why hadn't he noticed earlier?

"Of course . . . that's why she loves Chris Black's novels. When she confessed as much to me, she wasn't talking about Chris Black, she was talking about Eva Simplon. There is no doubt about it: Sylvie is a lesbian!"

He saw his cousin's life before him as if he were leafing through a photo album at great speed: her excessive infatuation with a father who would have rather had a boy, her doomed love affairs and failed relationships with men no one ever met—whereas at every birthday party for the last fifty years all her friends came, all of them girls . . . That afternoon, the three women she had run into so enthusiastically—a rather suspicious enthusiasm, no?—didn't they all, with their short boyish hair, their masculine clothes, their graceless way of moving, look like Eva Simplon's boss in the novel, Josépha Katz, the fleshy dyke who hung around lesbian nightclubs in Los Angeles and drove a Chevrolet while smoking a cigar? Obviously . . .

Maurice clucked. The discovery only disconcerted him because it came so late.

"She could have told me. She should have told me. I can understand things like that. We'll talk about it tomorrow if . . ."

Those were his last thoughts before he drifted into unconsciousness.

Alas, the following day did not go as he planned. Sylvie, grateful to her cousin for inaugurating their stay by accepting her modest evening by the television, suggested a cultural excursion: with a guidebook in her hand, she had put together an itinerary that would enable them to visit prehistoric caves and Romanesque churches. Maurice didn't have the nerve to protest, particularly as he couldn't see himself confessing to what was his sole desire: to stay home and read Chris Black.

Between two chapels, while he was walking along the fortified walls of a medieval village, he decided to tackle the problem from another angle, by telling the truth.

"Tell me, Sylvie, if I were to tell you I was a homosexual, would you be shocked?"

"Oh, my God, Maurice, are you gay?"

"No, I'm not."

"Well then why are you asking me?"

"Just to let you know that I wouldn't be shocked, if I were to learn you were a lesbian."

Her face went bright red. She could not catch her breath.

"What are you saying, Maurice?"

"I just wanted to say, that when you truly love someone, you can accept everything."

"Yes, I agree."

"So, you can confide in me, Sylvie."

From bright red, she went to dark violet. It took her a minute before she could carry on.

"Do you think I'm hiding something from you, Maurice?"

"Yes, I do."

They walked on for another hundred yards or so then she stopped, turned to face him and said in a tearful voice, "You're right. I am hiding something from you, but it's still too early."

"I'm here to listen."

Maurice's confident composure seemed to upset his cousin, and she could no longer keep back her tears.

"I . . . I . . . didn't expect that from you . . . That's . . . It's wonderful . . ."

He smiled, the good prince.

At dinner, after a succulent *magret de canard,* he tried to broach the subject again.

"Tell me, your friends—Grace, Gina, and—"

"Grace, Audrey, and Sofia."

"Have you known them for a long time?"

"No. Not very long. A few months."

"Really? And yet yesterday you seemed very close."

"Sometimes there are things that bring people together."

"Where did you meet them?"

"It's . . . it's awkward . . . I'd rather not . . ."

"It's too early?"

"It's too early."

"When you're ready."

A lesbian night club, like the one in the novel, it had to be! Something like L'Ambigu or The Kitty that Coughs, the sort of nightclub where Josépha Katz would go to pick up women . . . Sylvie didn't dare confess. Maurice concluded that he had behaved perfectly with his cousin, and that henceforth he deserved to go and lose himself in the book he had pilfered from her.

According to the same script as the night before, he switched on the television, pretended to be interested in an inane series, then lowered his jaw as if sleep were attacking him, and finally went to take refuge upstairs.

As soon as he was in his bedroom, he took just enough time to brush his teeth and hide the base of the door, then he rushed to pick up the book.

From her very first sentence Eva Simplon was brilliant, and gave Maurice the impression that she had been moping all day long waiting for him to return. In a few seconds, he was back in Darkwell, Aunt Agatha's mysterious demesne, dangerously isolated deep in the mountains. He trembled at the thought of the chanting that emerged every night from its walls.

This time, he was so absorbed by the novel that he did not hear Sylvie switch off the television and go to bed. It was only at midnight that a sinister hooting tore him from his pages, and he lifted his head.

The owl!

Or the man who was imitating the owl!

He clenched his teeth.

He waited for a few minutes.

Again, the cry.

This time, however, there'd be no dithering: this was no animal cry, this was a human cry.

A shiver went down his neck: the door!

Sylvie had probably not locked the doors and windows tonight, any more than yesterday. Particularly as in the morning, he had gotten up before her, and had opened the shutters to avoid any questions.

Above all, he must not yield to panic. Keep his cool. Show more self-control than he had yesterday.

He switched off his light, removed the comforter from the bottom of the door, and went down the stairs trying not to let the wooden steps creak.

Breathe deeply. One. Two. One. Two.

When he got down to the landing, what he saw paralyzed him with fright.

Too late!

A man was treading slowly through the living room in the slanting rays of the moon. On the walls, his gigantic shadow was even more impressive, defining a sharp chin, a heavy jaw, and curiously pointed ears. Silent, meticulous, he was lifting every cushion, every Afghan, blindly groping on shelves.

Maurice held his breath. The intruder's calm terrified him as much as his presence. In flashes, the mercury light illuminated his bald head, as smooth as a bonze's. The colossus did not bump into any of the furniture or the sofas, as if he already knew the house, and he went on feeling his way around the premises, exploring the same spots two or three times. What was he looking for?

The burglar's professional poise was contagious. Maurice hovered in the shadow and did not shake, nor did he panic. In any case, what could he do? Switch on the light to frighten him? It was not a light bulb that would get rid of him . . . call Sylvie? Nor a woman . . . Rush up to him, knock him over, and tie him up? This athletic looking man would have the upper hand. And besides, maybe he had a weapon. A pistol, or a knife . . .

Maurice swallowed so noisily that he was afraid he might suddenly betray his presence.

The intruder did not react.

Maurice hoped he was exaggerating the volume of the sounds his body was making; just now, for example, this crazy rumbling in his stomach . . .

The intruder let out a sigh. He couldn't find what he had come for.

Was he going to go upstairs? Maurice had the feeling that if he did, his own heart would stop.

The stranger hesitated, his powerful face raised to the ceiling, then, as if giving up, he went out the door.

His steps resonated at the front of the house.

After he'd gone a few yards, the crunching sound stopped.

Was he waiting? Was he going to come back?

How should Maurice react?

Should he throw himself against the door, and turn the key twice? The colossus would notice, come back, and burst through the French windows.

It would be best to wait and see if he went away.

And make doubly sure.

Maurice went cautiously back up the stairs and into his room, closed the door, and went over to the window.

He couldn't see very well through the narrow slits between the closed shutters. The strip of dense, deserted scrub that he could just make out was not enough for him to conclude that the intruder had left.

Maurice stayed frozen for an hour, watching, listening. At times it seemed to him that nothing was moving, but at other times he believed it was starting up again. This vast house already made such a racket just by itself—beams cracking, floors creaking, pipes groaning, mice scampering in the attic— that it was hard to identify all these muffled activities.

But he would have to go back down. He could not possibly spend the night with the door and the shutters open! The man might come back. If he had refrained from going upstairs, it was because he knew that people were living there; but he might change his mind. He might come back later, assuming everyone was asleep, to look for what he wanted on the second floor. And anyway, what was he looking for?

"No, Maurice, don't be stupid, don't mix this up with the book you're reading: unlike *The Chamber of Dark Secrets,* this house surely does not conceal a manuscript containing the list of all the children Christ and Mary Magdalene had together. You must not get worked up. However, there is something here, some unique thing that this unknown colossus wants, there's something he's looking for and not for the first time either, because he moves around so easily in here . . . what could it be?"

The floor in the corridor vibrated.

Was the intruder coming back?

On his knees, Maurice slid over to the door and looked through the keyhole.

Phew, it was Sylvie.

The moment he opened the door, his cousin jumped.

"Maurice, you're not in bed? Maybe I woke you up . . ."

Maurice uttered in a toneless voice, "Why are you up? Did you see anything?"

"Excuse me?"

"Did you notice anything abnormal?"

"No . . . I . . . I couldn't sleep, so I thought I might fix myself some herbal tea. I'm sorry. Did I frighten you?"

"No, no . . ."

"What then? Did you see something strange?"

Sylvie's eyes grew large with fear.

Maurice hesitated about what to answer. No, best not to panic her. Play for time first. Play for time against the intruder, who might come back.

"Tell me, Sylvie," he said, trying to make his words sound normal and come out regularly, "wouldn't it be better to close the shutters at night? And the door, I'm sure you didn't lock it."

"Bah, what's there to be afraid of, nobody wanders around up here. Just remember how hard it was even to find the road."

Maurice thought that she was lucky to be so silly. If he told her that not even an hour ago, a stranger was going around sizing up the living room . . . It would be better if she went on wallowing in her trusting ignorance. He himself would be less afraid if he was the only one who was afraid.

She came up and looked at him.

"Have you seen something?"

"No."

"Anything out of the ordinary?"

"No. I'm simply suggesting we close the door and the shutters. Is that really unthinkable for you? Against your principles? Is your religion opposed to it? You find it such a radical step? You won't sleep at night if we lock ourselves in? Will you be in the throes of insomnia if we take the most basic safety precautions, which is why locks and shutters were invented?"

Sylvie noticed that her cousin was losing control over his nerves. She gave him a bracing smile.

"No, of course not. I'll help you with it. Better still, I'll do it for you."

Maurice sighed: at least he wouldn't have to go back out into the night where the colossus was prowling.

"Thank you. Here, I'll make your tea for you in the meanwhile."

They went downstairs. When Maurice saw how nonchalantly she took her time outside to close the shelters, he blessed her for being so utterly unaware.

After she had turned the key twice in the door, and rammed home the bolts, she joined him in the kitchen.

"Do you remember how frightened you used to be when you were little?"

Maurice was annoyed by her words, that seemed uncalled for.

"I wasn't frightened, I was cautious."

His answer had nothing to do with the past, and everything to do with the present situation. What did it matter! Sylvie, astonished by her cousin's sudden authority, did not quibble.

While her lime-blossom tea was steeping, she reminisced about their childhood vacations, their boat outings while the adults were plunged deep in their siesta on the banks of the Rhône, the fish they stole from the fishermen's pots to let them go again in the river, the cabin they had called the Lighthouse on an island that divided the waters . . .

While Sylvie followed the thread of her nostalgia, memory was leading Maurice elsewhere, to other memories of that time, when his parents began once again to go out dancing, or to the movies, being of the mind that their ten-year-old son was reasonable enough now to stay by himself in the apartment. He lived through hours of terror. Abandoned, a tiny boy beneath vast ceilings twelve feet high, he would scream, missing his mother and father, their familiar presence, their reassuring smells, the melody of their consoling words; he wept copiously, because his body knew that tears were a way to make his parents come to him. To no avail. What had worked for years to rescue him from helplessness and pain and solitude no longer had the slightest effect. He had lost all his power. He was no longer a child. And not yet an adult. Moreover, when they came back, at one o'clock in the morning—lively, joyful, drunk, their voices different, their smells different, their gestures different— he hated them and swore that he would never grow up to become an adult like them, a sensual, lascivious, cocky adult who loved the pleasures of food and wine and flesh. And while he had matured, it was in a different way, by developing his mind. Cerebral pursuits, science, culture, erudition. No food, and no sex. He may have become an adult, but by becoming a scholar, not by becoming an animal.

Is that why he had always refused to read novels? Because on those evenings when she betrayed him, his mother left the books she loved on the night table to keep him busy? Or was it because he blindly believed everything in the first one he read, and he felt humiliated when his parents, dying of laughter, informed him that it was all made up?

"Maurice . . . Maurice . . . are you listening? I'm finding you a bit strange."

"But everything is strange, Sylvie. Everything. Strange and foreign. Look, you and me, we've known each other since birth, and yet are both keeping secrets from each other."

"Are you referring to—"

"I am referring to what you are not talking about, that you might, some day, talk about."

"I swear to you I will talk about it."

She flung her arms around him, hugged him, then immediately felt embarrassed by her gesture.

"Goodnight, Maurice. See you in the morning."

The following day was so strange and unexpected that neither one of them had the strength to talk about it.

Maurice had initially been tempted to go back to sleep after all the excitement then, because he didn't manage to, he switched the light back on and went on reading *The Chamber of Dark Secrets*. His sensitive nature, already greatly tested by the intruder's visit, did not recover its calm anywhere in the rest of the novel: Eva Simplon—how he admired this woman, you could really count on her—was being threatened by unscrupulous buyers orchestrating deadly incidents because she refused to sell Darkwell. Every time, she just barely managed to make it out alive from an assassination attempt disguised as an accident. And every time, Eva Simplon found herself up against a new problem, just as worrying: she could not find the entrance to the esoteric room where the nightly chanting was coming from. She felt her way along all the walls, inspected the cellar, and examined the attic, but found nothing. She studied the surveyors' map at the town hall, and the analysis of successive blueprints in the archives at a notary's led her to believe that there must be a body inside the building. How could she reach it? Who was getting in there every night? Eva refused to believe in ghosts or spirits. Fortunately, that bitch of a Josépha Katz had sent her a young architect who was trying to analyze the structure of the house—and while Josépha Katz may have been an infernal dyke who was still hitting on Eva Simplon, despite being rebuffed umpteen times, she turned out to be extremely professional—because maybe he would discover an explanation that would eliminate any supernatural hypotheses. And yet . . . in short, at eight o'clock in the morning, Maurice, who hadn't had any rest at all, got up, tired and irritable, and furious at having to leave Eva Simplon in Darkwell and find himself abruptly in the Ardèche with his cousin. All the more so because today, Monday, he was going to have to put up with a picnic with the girlfriends from the supermarket . . . a day spent in a lesbian colony, among these women who were all more solidly built and manly than he was, no thank you!

He tried to argue that he didn't feel well and would rather stay home and look after himself. Sylvie would not back down.

"It's out of the question. If you're sick and it gets serious, I have to stay here and pamper you. So either I stay here, or you come with me."

Sorely aware that he would not manage to rescue his day for reading, he went with her.

The hours that followed were a torture. A sadistic sun beat down on the rocky path they walked along to exhaustion. When they reached a green reservoir where the Ardèche river flowed calmly after its torrential flood, Maurice found himself unable to dip any more than one little toe in the icy water. The lunch in the grass turned into a trap because Maurice started off by sitting on an anthill full of red ants and then was stung by a bee that wanted to share his apricot. He emptied his lungs until his head was spinning in order to keep the fire going to cook the sausages; the rest of the afternoon, he had difficulty digesting his hard-boiled egg.

Back at the house, the women wanted to play a party game. Thinking he was safe at last, Maurice was about to sneak off for a refreshing siesta, but when he learned it was a contest based on historical and geographical knowledge, he couldn't resist, and joined in after all. He won every round, and this compelled him to continue, and the more victories he won, the more condescending he became toward his partners. When he became too despicable, the women got fed up, and aperitifs were served. Pastis on top of a day in the sun was all that was needed to upset his fragile balance, so that by the time he and Sylvie went back inside the villa not only was he aching all over, but he had a stubborn headache.

At nine o'clock, the moment he had taken his last bite, he locked all the shutters and the door and went up to bed.

Leaning on his pillows, he hesitated between two contradictory feelings: the delight of being with Eva Simplon once again, and the dread of a new visit from the intruder. After a few pages, he forgot his dilemma, and was trembling in unison with the heroine.

At ten thirty, he could hear Sylvie switching off the television and climbing heavily up the stairs.

At eleven o'clock, he was beginning, like Eva Simplon, to wonder whether, basically, ghosts existed or not. Otherwise, how could you explain that individuals could walk through walls? There comes a time when what is irrational ceases to be irrational, because it becomes the only rational solution.

At half past eleven, a noise roused him abruptly from his book.

Footsteps. Lights, discreet footsteps. Not at all Sylvie's footsteps.

He switched off the light and went over to the door. Moving the comforter to one side, he turned the knob. He could sense a presence on the ground floor.

No sooner did this thought cross his mind than the man appeared in the stairway. The bald colossus, treading cautiously and silently, coming upstairs to continue his search.

Maurice closed his door and leaned against the woodwork to resist any attempt the intruder might make to come in. In the fraction of a second, his body was soaked, he was sweating thick drops that he could feel trickling down his neck and his back.

The stranger stopped by his door then continued on his way.

With his ear up against the wood, Maurice could hear a rustling noise that confirmed the man was heading down the hall.

Sylvie! He was going into Sylvie's room!

What should he do? Run away! Rush down the stairs and get the hell out of there, into the night. But where? Maurice didn't know the surrounding countryside, whereas the intruder knew every bend in the road. Besides, he couldn't sacrifice his cousin like some coward and leave her to the hands of this miscreant . . .

He cracked the door and saw the shadow go into Sylvie's room.

"If I stop to think any more, I won't move."

He had to hurry! Maurice knew very well that with each passing second he was losing his ability to take any initiative.

"Remember, Maurice, it's like diving from the high board: if you don't jump right away, you'll never jump. Your salvation lies the way of unconsciousness."

He took a deep breath and leapt out into the corridor. He rushed toward the bedroom.

"Sylvie, watch out! Watch out!"

As the intruder had closed the door, Maurice bashed it open.

"Get out!"

The room was empty.

Quickly! Under the bed!

Maurice went flat on the ground. No strangers were hiding under the bed.

Closet! Clothes cupboard! Quickly!

In a few seconds, he opened all the doors.

As he could not understand what was going on, he screamed, "Sylvie! Sylvie, where are you?"

The door to the bathroom opened, Sylvie came out, with a look of panic, her bathrobe hardly tied, holding a brush in her hand.

"What's going on?"

"Are you alone in the bathroom?"

"Maurice, have you lost your mind?"

"Are you alone in the bathroom?"

Docile, she went back in, looked around, then frowned to indicate her bewilderment.

"Well, obviously, I'm alone in my bathroom. Who should I be with?"

Devastated, Maurice collapsed on the edge of the bed. Sylvie rushed over to take him in her arms.

"Maurice, what is going on? Did you have a nightmare? Speak to me, Maurice, speak to me, tell me what's worrying you."

From that very moment, he had to keep quiet, otherwise, like Eva Simplon in the novel, they would think he had gone insane, and would pretend to listen to him without hearing him.

"I . . . I . . ."

"Yes, tell me, Maurice. Tell me."

"I . . . I must've had a nightmare."

"There, there, it's over. Everything is fine. It was nothing serious. Come on, we'll go down to the kitchen and I'll make us some tea."

She led him downstairs, constantly talking, confident, unruffled, imperturbable. Maurice, progressively won over by her serenity, thought he was right to keep his fears to himself. Sylvie's tranquil attitude would give him the strength to conduct the investigation right to the end. After all, he was nothing but a simple history teacher, not an agent from the FBI, used to exceptional situations the way Eva Simplon was.

While Sylvie was babbling, he wondered if there wasn't an analogy between this house and Darkwell. A secret room with a trap door might even be hidden behind these walls, a hideout where the intruder might have found refuge.

He shuddered.

That meant the intruder was still among them . . . wouldn't it be better if they left right away?

A sudden revelation overwhelmed him. Of course! How obvious! How could the man have gotten in here since all the access from outside had been blocked off?

He hadn't come in: he already was in. In fact, the man lived in this place, and had lived here longer than they had. He was living in a space they had not discovered because of the rather strange architecture.

"We disturbed him when we arrived."

Who is he? And what is he looking for at night?

Unless . . .

No . . . .

Yes! Why couldn't it be a ghost? After all, people have been talking about ghosts for so long. As Josépha Katz declared between two puffs on her cigar, there's no smoke without fire. What if . . .

Maurice, taken aback, could not determine which was more terrifying, the colossus hiding somewhere inside the house without them knowing how or why, or a ghost haunting the house . . .

"Maurice, I'm worried about you. You don't seem to be yourself."

"Hmm? Maybe I've got a bit of sunstroke . . ."

"Maybe . . . Tomorrow, if you don't feel better, I'll call the doctor."

Maurice thought, "Tomorrow, we'll be dead," but kept it to himself.

"Well, I'm going back to bed."

"Do you want some more tea?"

"No, thank you, Sylvie. Go ahead of me, please." While Sylvie was going up the first steps, Maurice used the pretext of switching off the lights in the kitchen to grab a long carving knife from a hook on the wall. He slipped it up into his loose pajama sleeve.

Upstairs, they wished each other sweet dreams.

Maurice was about to close his door again when Sylvie stopped him, turning her cheek to him.

"Here, I feel like a goodnight kiss. That way, you'll be even calmer."

She left a damp kiss on his temple. Just as she stepped back, her eyes filled with surprise: she saw something behind Maurice, yes, something in the room that was alarming her!

"What? What is it?" he exclaimed, panicking, convinced the intruder must be standing behind him.

Sylvie thought for a moment and then burst out laughing.

"No, I was just thinking about something else, no connection. Stop being so worried like this, Maurice, you're getting yourself all in a tizzy. Everything is fine."

She went away, laughing.

Maurice watched her disappear with a mixture of envy and pity. Ignorance is bliss! She doesn't suspect a thing, and she even laughs at my anxiety. Maybe there is a ghost or a potential murderer just behind the wall where she leans her pillows, and she would rather tease me. Be a hero, Maurice, leave her to her illusions: don't let it annoy you.

He lay down to think, but his meditation only managed to make him more worried than ever. Particularly as the unusual presence of the knife with its shiny blade lying next to his thigh on the sheet frightened him more than it stimulated him.

He opened up *The Chamber of Dark Secrets* once again, as if he were coming home after a particularly trying journey. Maybe he would find the solution in the book?

At one o'clock in the morning, when the story was more suspenseful than ever, and he only had fifty pages left to find the solution to the puzzle, he sensed something moving in the corridor.

This time, without hesitating for a second, he switched off the light, and took hold of the handle of his weapon beneath the sheet.

A few seconds later, the doorknob began to turn, a fraction of an inch at a time.

The intruder was trying to come into his room.

With a great deal of caution, and nerve-racking slowness, he opened the door. When he had crossed the threshold, the gray light from the lantern in the corridor shone on his bald head.

Maurice held his breath, and pretended to close his eyes; he kept them open a crack to follow the movements of the colossus.

He came up to Maurice's bed and reached out his hand.

"He's going to strangle me!"

Maurice sprang out of the sheets, with a knife in his hand and, screaming with terror, struck the stranger, splattering his blood.

There was an unusual amount of activity. In fact, such events were very rare in these sleepy provincial villages, ordinarily so quiet.

Alongside the police cars were those of the mayor, the local parliamentary deputy, and the nearest neighbors. While the house overlooked a rocky wilderness, dozens of rubberneckers had managed to hear about the incident and had come running.

They were obliged to limit access to the villa by means of a symbolic gate—plastic tape—and by stationing three gendarmes to ward off any unhealthy curiosity.

While a truck was removing the corpse, the policemen and the authorities looked unconvinced while the massive woman repeated her story for the tenth time, stumbling over her own words to hiccup, weep, and blow her nose.

"Please, at least let my friends in. Oh, here they are."

Grace, Audrey, and Sophia rushed up to Sylvie to hug her and console her. Then they sat down on the next sofa.

Sylvie justified their presence to the policemen.

"It is through them that I rented this villa. We met this winter at the hospital where we were being treated, in Professor Millau's service. Oh, my God, if I had even suspected . . ."

She began to tell her story again for her friends.

"I can't understand what happened. He was so kind, Maurice, this year. More easy-going than the other times. Simpler. I think he had understood that I was recovering from a sickness, that I'd had chemotherapy for my cancer. Maybe someone told him? Or did he guess? All these last days, he kept reaching out to me, suggesting he loved me the way I was, that I needn't try to hide anything from him. But it's true that for me it's hard. Hard to accept that I've lost my hair because of the treatments, and that I have to hide my skull under a wig. The first night, I was sure he had seen me downstairs, in my pajamas, without my wig, I was looking for a book I had bought at the supermarket and had mislaid somewhere. Yesterday evening when I wished him good night at his door, after we had some tea, I realized that the damn book was in his room, on his bed. So around midnight, as I was tossing and turning and couldn't sleep—I've had trouble recuperating since my illness—I figured that I could go and get it from his room without disturbing him. Maurice was dozing. I was careful not to wake him up, I made my way without any noise, and just as I was about to put my hand on the book, he threw himself on me. I felt a terrible pain, and I saw a knife blade, and I cried out and fought him off, and sent him sprawling backwards, and he bounced against the wall and then fell on his side and then, shlack, the rabbit punch! His neck hit the night table! Stone dead!"

She had to stop for her sobs.

The police commissioner was rubbing his chin, unconvinced, then he conferred with his team. The hypothesis of an accident seemed improbable. Why would the man sleep with a knife unless he was afraid of his cousin attacking him?

Then, although the women protested in support of their friend, he informed Sylvie that she was under arrest. Not only was there no trace of a struggle but she was, according to her own confession, the victim's sole heir. She was taken away, her wrists in handcuffs.

The police commissioner went back upstairs by himself, his hands protected by gloves, and into transparent plastic bags he slipped the two exhibits: a huge kitchen knife, and a book, *The*

Chamber of Dark Secrets, by Chris Black, its pages also splattered with blood.

As he was closing the plastic around the book, he read beneath the brown smudges what you could still see of the description on the back, and he could not help but murmur with a sigh, "Some people really do read the trashiest stuff . . ."

THE WOMAN
WITH THE BOUQUET

At the train station in Zurich, on platform number three, there is a woman who has been waiting, every day for fifteen years, with a bouquet in her hand.

In the beginning, I didn't want to believe it. I had already made several journeys to see Egon Ammann, my German language publisher, before I noticed her; then it took me a long time to formulate my surprise, because the elderly lady looked so normal, so dignified, so noble, that you paid her no attention whatsoever. She was dressed in a black woolen suit with a long skirt, and wore flat shoes and dark stockings; an umbrella with a knob sculpted in the shape of a duck's beak emerged from her handbag of cuir-bouilli; a mother of pearl barrette held her hair in a chignon against her head, while a modest bouquet of wildflowers, with a dominant orange note, made a small splash of color in her gloved hands. There was nothing that suggested she might be a madwoman or an eccentric, so I had attributed my encounters with her to chance.

One spring, however, Ulla, one of Ammann's colleagues, met me on the platform by my carriage, so I pointed out the strange woman.

"It's very odd, I think I've seen this woman more than once. What a coincidence! She must be waiting for my double, someone who always takes the same train that I do and at the same time."

"Not at all," exclaimed Ulla, "she stands there every day and she waits."

"Who for?"

"Someone who doesn't come . . . because she goes away again every evening, alone, and comes back again the following day."

"Really! How long has this been going on?"

"Well, I've been seeing her for five years but I spoke with a stationmaster who says he noticed her at least fifteen years ago!"

"Are you making fun of me, Ulla? This sounds like a novel!"

Ulla blushed—the slightest emotion turned her crimson—then she stammered, laughed in confusion, and shook her head.

"I swear, it's true. Every day. For fifteen years. In fact, it must be more than fifteen years, because each of us has taken years to notice her presence . . . So the stationmaster must have as well . . . For example, you've been coming to Zurich for three years and you've only mentioned her today. Maybe she's been waiting for twenty or thirty years . . . She's never replied to anyone who asked what she was waiting for."

"She's right," I concluded. "Besides, who could answer such a question?"

We could not elucidate the matter any further, because we had to turn our attention to a series of interviews with the press.

I didn't think about it again until my next trip. The moment "Zurich" was announced over the train's loudspeakers, I recalled the woman with the bouquet and wondered, will she, yet again . . .

She was there, vigilant, on platform number three.

I looked at her closely. Light eyes, almost the color of mercury, on the verge of fading away. Pale but healthy skin, marked by the expressive claw of time. A thin body, still in good shape, that must once have been nimble and vigorous. The stationmaster was exchanging a few words with her, and she was nodding, smiling amiably, and then she went on her way, imperturbably, staring at the railroad lines. I was able to note only one eccentricity: a folding canvas seat, that she carried with her. Or was that the sign, rather, of a practical nature?

As soon as I arrived at the Ammann Verlag, after changing trams several times, I decided to conduct an investigation.

"Ulla, if you please, I must find out more about the woman with the bouquet."

Her cheeks went raspberry.

"As I was sure you would ask me again, I've come prepared. I went to the station and chatted with a few members of the staff, and now I've become very friendly with the man who runs the left luggage."

Well aware myself of how easy it was to like Ulla, I had no doubt that she had managed to extract as much information as possible. Although she can be abrupt, and slightly authoritarian, with a piercing gaze as she looks at her interlocutors, she offsets her rather strict approach with an explosive sense of humor, and the sort of joviality one would not expect from someone with such dark features. If she befriends everybody easily, it is because she is basically well-disposed toward people—and irrepressibly curious as well.

"Even though she spends her days outside on the platform, the woman with the bouquet is anything but a tramp. She lives in a fine bourgeois house, in a leafy street. She lives alone, with the daily help of a Turkish woman in her fifties. Her name is Frau Steinmetz."

"Frau Steinmetz? Will the Turkish woman tell us who she's waiting for at the station?"

"The Turkish woman hurries away the minute you go up to her. This I found out from a friend who lives in a neighboring street: the maid speaks neither German, French, nor Italian."

"Then how does she communicate with her mistress?"

"In Russian."

"The Turkish woman speaks Russian?"

"As does Frau Steinmetz."

"This is all very intriguing, Ulla. Were you able to find out this Frau Steinmetz's marital status?"

"I tried. I wasn't able to find anything."

"A husband? Children? Parents?"

"Nothing. Let me be precise: I can't swear she doesn't or didn't have a husband, or children, I only am saying that I don't know."

At teatime, over some *macarons*, the employees and the publisher Egon Ammann himself came to join us, and I brought up the subject once again.

"In your opinion, who is she waiting for, the woman with the bouquet?"

"Her son," answered Claudia. "A mother is always hoping that her son will come."

"Why her son?" asked Nelly, annoyed, "Why not her daughter!"

"Her husband," said Doris.

"Her lover," amended Rita.

"Her sister?" suggested Mathias.

In actual fact each of them, in their answer, was telling their own story. Claudia suffered from not seeing her son, who was a professor in Berlin; Nelly's daughter was married to a New Zealander; Doris was pining for her husband, a sales representative constantly away on business; Rita changed her lover as often as her underwear; as for young Mathias, he was a pacifist and a conscientious objector, doing his civil service by working rather than serving in the army, and clearly he was nostalgic for his family cocoon.

Ulla looked at her colleagues as if they were all mentally retarded.

"None of that, she's waiting for someone who died and she can't accept the fact."

"That doesn't change a thing," exclaimed Claudia. "It can still be her son."

"Her daughter."

"Her husband."

"Her lover."

"Her sister."

"Or a twin brother who died at birth," suggested the laconic, solitary Romy.

We looked at her: was this her own secret she was entrusting us with, if not that of the lady with the bouquet? She always seemed so sad.

To try another tack, I turned to Egon Ammann.

"And you, Egon, who do you think she is waiting for?"

Even though he kept company with us, Egon never said a great deal during these breaks, which he must have found childish. He is a passionate man, with intelligent eyebrows, a distinguished nose, he's read everything, and deciphered everything for sixty years, getting up at five o'clock in the morning to light his first cigarette and attack his pile of manuscripts, plowing through novels, devouring essays. It is as if his very long white hair were carrying the traces of an adventurous life—the wind from the countries he has seen, the smoke from the tons of tobacco he has burned, the dreams contained in the books he's published. So although he professes nothing, and does not moralize, he impresses me with his constant curiosity, his appetite for discovery, his gift for languages; next to him I feel like an amateur.

Egon shrugged, looking out the window at the great tits fluttering on the blossoming linden tree, and said, "Her first love?"

Then, embarrassed by his confession, furious at such a slip, he frowned and gave me a harsh stare.

"And what's your theory, Eric?"

"A first love who will never return," I murmured.

There was a silence in the room. We had all understood the trap. Through this unknown woman, we had divulged our most private wishes, confessing the very thing that we were waiting for, or could wait for, in our deepest soul. How I would have liked to be able to get inside their skulls, to know them better.

And yet, how greatly I appreciated the fact that they did not get into mine. What a painful place it is, this brain of mine, this enclosure of unvoiced words, this dark sanctuary guarded by my temples! There are certain words I could not utter without collapsing. How much better to keep silent. Do we not all find our depth in our silence?

Back at home, I went on thinking about the woman with the bouquet. On subsequent trips to Zurich I traveled by car or plane, and I did not have the opportunity to go through the station.

A year or two went by.

What was odd about that woman with the bouquet was that I forgot her without forgetting her, or rather I thought about her at times when I felt somewhat lonely, at times when it was impossible to question anyone . . . Her image haunted only those moments of helplessness. Nevertheless, I did manage, one day when I was talking to Ulla on the telephone, to bring her up again.

"Yes, yes, I assure you: she's still there. Every day. Platform number three. To be sure, she's beginning to look tired; from time to time, she dozes off, sitting on her seat, but then she gets a hold of herself, and she picks up her bouquet and looks up and down the platform."

"She fascinates me."

"I can't see why. Although she doesn't look it, she is surely just out of her mind, an unfortunate madwoman. Besides, nowadays, with cell phones and the Internet, you don't go and greet someone on a station platform, do you?"

"What interests me, it's not *why* she's waiting on the platform, but *who* she's waiting for. Who can you be waiting for like that, for years, or even your entire life?"

"Beckett, waiting for Godot."

"A sham! For him, the point was to show that the world is absurd, that there's no God, and that we are wrong to promise ourselves anything in this life. Beckett's a street cleaner, he'll sweep earth and sky and send all your hope—stinking refuse—to the dump. What I find interesting about the woman with the bouquet is that there are two questions she inspires. The first one: who are we waiting for? The second: is it right or wrong to wait?"

"Here, I'm going to hand the receiver to the boss, he's been listening to our conversation. He's got something to read to you."

"Eric? Just one sentence for you. 'What is interesting in an enigma is not the truth that it hides, but the mystery that it contains.'"

"Thank you for the quotation, Egon."

I hung up, fully suspecting that on the other end of the line they must be laughing at me.

Last spring, I went once again by train to Zurich to give a lecture. Obviously, the moment I climbed into the carriage, I could think of no one but her. I was looking forward to seeing her again, peaceful, smiling, faithful, indifferent to everyone, attentive to something we knew nothing about. She was a woman we had only glimpsed for a few seconds, and yet we spoke about her for hours, as if she were a sphinx hiding a secret, an inexhaustible ferment for our imagination.

As we came into Zurich, I mused that there was one certain thing we knew: she was not waiting for any of us. Could it be that our silence, our disinclination to probe further, our intermittent forgetfulness were all rooted there, in that humiliation, the fact that she looked right through us as if we were all invisible?

"Zurich!"

As I stepped down on the platform I noticed her absence at once. A few bystanders had just left platform number three behind them—a spotless, empty space.

What had happened to her?

As I went through Zurich on the tram, I refused to indulge in hypotheses. Ulla must know, Ulla knew, Ulla would tell me. So I concentrated on looking out at this unusual city, both rich and modest, a grandmother's dream, where buildings seem to have been constructed for the sake of the geraniums beaming down from windowsills, a peaceful town as sleepy as the lake resting against its side; while behind its thick walls, deals are being made with powerful economic consequences. Zurich has always seemed mysterious to me because of its absence of mystery: while we Latins think that anything that is dirty, meandering and profuse is adventurous, Zurich is well behaved, clean, and neatly ordered, yet it becomes strange for its very—extreme—lack of strangeness. It has the charm of an elegant lover, wearing a bow tie and tux, the exemplary son, the ideal son-in-law, yet it is capable of committing the worst debauchery the moment the door is closed.

At the Ammann Verlag, I got my chores out of the way—discussions, program—then I made the most of a break to go and speak to Ulla between two doors.

"What happened to the woman with the bouquet?"

She rolled her eyes, aghast.

"As soon as we get a minute, I'll tell you."

In the evening, after the lecture, book signing, and dinner, we went back to the hotel, exhausted. Without saying a word, we sat down at the bar and pointed to the cocktails we wanted, then I switched off my cell phone while Ulla lit a cigarette.

"Well?" I asked.

I had no need to be more specific. She knew what I was waiting for.

"The woman with the bouquet was waiting for something, and whatever that something was, it came. That's why she isn't there anymore."

"What happened?"

"My friend at the left luggage told me everything. Three

weeks ago, the woman with the bouquet suddenly got up, radiant, her eyes full of wonder. She waved in the direction of a man getting out of the carriage, and he saw her right away. She threw her arms around him. They embraced for a long time. Even the baggage handlers were moved, she radiated so much happiness. The man was tall, wearing a long, dark coat, and no one recognized him because a felt hat partially hid his features; from what they were able to tell me about him, he didn't seem at all surprised to see her there. They left the station arm in arm. At the last minute, she did something rather whimsical: she left her canvas seat on the ground, as if it didn't belong to her. Oh, I nearly forgot the strangest detail: the man was traveling without a suitcase, and the only thing he had to carry was the orange bouquet she had given him."

"And then?"

"My friend who's a neighbor told me the rest. Did I mention him? He lives one street over from Frau Steinmetz."

"Yes, yes. Go on, please."

"That evening, the man went with her into the house. She ordered her maid to go out and to only come back the next day. An order which the Turkish woman duly obeyed."

"And?"

"She didn't come back until the next day."

"And?"

"When she came in, the lady with the bouquet was dead."

"Pardon?"

"Dead. A natural death. Her heart had stopped."

"It couldn't have been the man . . ."

"No. There was no doubt about it. The doctors confirmed she'd had a heart attack. He is completely innocent. Particularly as he—"

"Yes?"

"He had disappeared."

"What?"

"Whoosh. Gone! As if he had never been in the house at all. The Turkish woman claims she never saw him."

"And yet you just—"

"Yes. My neighbor friend testified that the man went in the house but the maid denies it, totally. In any case, the police aren't interested one way or the other, because there's nothing suspicious about her death. My friend is keeping quiet now because the more he insisted, the more the neighborhood took him for a cretin."

We sank further into our leather armchairs and started on our cocktails. We thought for a moment.

"So there's no trace of him? No information about him?"

"None at all."

"Where did his train come from?"

"No one could tell me that."

We asked the barman for a second round, as if the alcohol might tame the mystery.

"Where is the Turkish woman?"

"Gone. Back to her country."

"And who inherited the villa?"

"The city."

So no motive of foul play could provide an explanation. A third round definitely was called for. The barman began to look at us with a worried air.

We were silent.

Ulla and I could make nothing more of the story, but we still enjoyed thinking about it. Ordinarily, life kills off stories like this: there are mornings when you feel that something is about to begin, something pure and rich and unique, then the telephone rings and it's all over. Life chops us up and scatters us, leaves us in fragments, refuses the clean brushstroke. What was special about the woman with the bouquet was that life took a certain shape again: her fate had all the purity of literature, the economy of a work of art.

At two o'clock, we left each other to go off to sleep, but sleep was slow in coming: until morning I sought to know who the woman with the bouquet was waiting for on platform number three at Zurich station.

And I think that until my very last day, I will wonder whether it was death, or love, that alighted from the train.

ABOUT THE AUTHOR

Eric-Emmanuel Schmitt, playwright, novelist, and author of short stories, was awarded the French Academy's Grand Prix du Théâtre in 2001. He is one of Europe's most popular authors. His books include *Oscar and the Lady in Pink* (1999), *The Gospel According to Pilate* (2000), and *The Most Beautiful Book in the World*, published by Europa Editions in 2009. The film *Odette Toulemonde*, Schmitt's debut as screenwriter and director, was released in 2007.

Carmine Abate
Between Two Seas
"A moving portrayal of generational continuity."
—*Kirkus*
224 pp • $14.95 • 978-1-933372-40-2

Salwa Al Neimi
The Proof of the Honey
"Al Neimi announces the end of a taboo in the Arab world:
that of *sex!*"
—*Reuters*
144 pp • $15.00 • 978-1-933372-68-6

Alberto Angela
A Day in the Life of Ancient Rome
"Fascinating and accessible."
—*Il Giornale*
392 pp • $16.00 • 978-1-933372-71-6

Muriel Barbery
The Elegance of the Hedgehog
"Gently satirical, exceptionally winning and inevitably bittersweet."
—Michael Dirda, *The Washington Post*
336 pp • $15.00 • 978-1-933372-60-0

Gourmet Rhapsody
"In the pages of this book, Barbery shows off her finest gift: lightness."
—*La Repubblica*
176 pp • $15.00 • 978-1-933372-95-2

Stefano Benni
Margherita Dolce Vita
"A modern fable...hilarious social commentary."—*People*
240 pp • $14.95 • 978-1-933372-20-4

Timeskipper
"Benni again unveils his Italian brand of magical realism."
—*Library Journal*
400 pp • $16.95 • 978-1-933372-44-0

Romano Bilenchi
The Chill
120 pp • $15.00 • 978-1-933372-90-7

Massimo Carlotto
The Goodbye Kiss
"A masterpiece of Italian noir."
—*Globe and Mail*
160 pp • $14.95 • 978-1-933372-05-1

Death's Dark Abyss
"A remarkable study of corruption and redemption."
—*Kirkus* (starred review)
160 pp • $14.95 • 978-1-933372-18-1

The Fugitive
"[Carlotto is] the reigning king of Mediterranean noir."
—*The Boston Phoenix*
176 pp • $14.95 • 978-1-933372-25-9

(with Marco Videtta)
Poisonville
"The business world as described by Carlotto and Videtta
in *Poisonville* is frightening as hell."
—*La Repubblica*
224 pp • $15.00 • 978-1-933372-91-4

Francisco Coloane
Tierra del Fuego
"Coloane is the Jack London of our times."—Alvaro Mutis
192 pp • $14.95 • 978-1-933372-63-1

Giancarlo De Cataldo
The Father and the Foreigner
"A slim but touching noir novel from one of Italy's best writers
in the genre."—*Quaderni Noir*
144 pp • $15.00 • 978-1-933372-72-3

Shashi Deshpande
The Dark Holds No Terrors
"[Deshpande is] an extremely talented storyteller."—*Hindustan Times*
272 pp • $15.00 • 978-1-933372-67-9

Helmut Dubiel
Deep In the Brain: Living with Parkinson's Disease
"A book that begs reflection."—*Die Zeit*
144 pp • $15.00 • 978-1-933372-70-9

Steve Erickson
Zeroville
"A funny, disturbing, daring and demanding novel—Erickson's best."
—*The New York Times Book Review*
352 pp • $14.95 • 978-1-933372-39-6

Elena Ferrante
The Days of Abandonment
"The raging, torrential voice of [this] author is something rare."
—*The New York Times*
192 pp • $14.95 • 978-1-933372-00-6

Troubling Love
"Ferrante's polished language belies the rawness of her imagery."
—*The New Yorker*
144 pp • $14.95 • 978-1-933372-16-7

The Lost Daughter
"So refined, almost translucent."—*The Boston Globe*
144 pp • $14.95 • 978-1-933372-42-6

Jane Gardam
Old Filth
"Old Filth belongs in the Dickensian pantheon of memorable characters."
—*The New York Times Book Review*
304 pp • $14.95 • 978-1-933372-13-6

The Queen of the Tambourine
"A truly superb and moving novel."—*The Boston Globe*
272 pp • $14.95 • 978-1-933372-36-5